MW01633640

Joan Soggie

Print ISBNs
Amazon Print 9780228620617
BWL Print 9780228620624
LSI Print 9780228620631

Dedication

This book is dedicated to my husband's grandmother, Henrikka Lund Sogge (1861-1931) and to her descendants, especially my husband, Dennis Soggie, and our children, Kimberly, Neil, Lori, and Andrea, their children, and grandchildren. They are my joy, and the reason for writing this story.

I wish to acknowledge Joan Carlson, who edited *From Nordic Roots: One Family's Journey,* an invaluable source of information. A shout out to the kind folks of Teulon, Manitoba who generously shared historical data. Thanks also to the good souls who back in the 1960s had the foresight to compile *Elbow Homestead Days 1898-1910*. That early Saskatchewan story would be lost if not for them.

My appreciation to Dorothy Bird and Mary Lu Foreman who read early drafts, and to Heather Macdonald and my editor at BWL Publishing for final editing.

Dates, family names, places, and historical events are based on fact; my depiction of those people and events is purely the product of my imagination.

Chapter One

Chicago, 1928

Gray clouds scudded across a gray sky. Rikka shivered at the window and pulled the shawl tight about her shoulders. Even in this overheated apartment, a chill wind seemed to penetrate her bones.

Kris had warned her. "Chicago is cold in November, Mama."

But not the clean sharp cold of the northern sea. Not the stubborn hard cold of the northern prairie. Here, the wind seems to carry dampness and disease.

Dis-ease. The absence or lack of ease or comfort. She played with the English word in her mind, carefully skirting the more obvious meaning. Being here in Chicago was hard enough. So far from every place she had called home. No need to make it unbearable by letting her mind dwell on the doctor's words. On illness. On death.

Rikka turned and stepped across the room into the tiny kitchenette. With some trepidation she turned on the gas, following the directions Kris had given her that morning.

"See, Mama, it's easy. Just turn this little dial, push this button, and presto, the burner lights. Then, when you want to shut it off, turn the dial back here. Tons easier than your old wood stove."

Easier, maybe. But so dangerous! But then fire is always dangerous.

The old pain rose in her throat, and she swallowed hard, pushing it down. Coffee would help. The coffee bread had cooled on the side counter. She sliced it now and arranged it on a plate, the one with red and blue flowers. *Like the little flowers that bloomed on the rocky hillside above the house at Karstenoya.* The coffee was perking now, its fragrance bringing cheeriness to the room. *Be sure to turn the dial, shut off the gas*, she reminded herself, and did so, pausing to watch the last few burps of black coffee fill the glass dome on the coffeepot lid. She reached high into the cupboard and got down the blue cups.

The doorbell buzzed. *Marianne is at least punctual.* Rikka smoothed her black skirt and brushed her hand over the still thick coil of gray hair - chignon, Torolf called it, but just the same smooth coiled braid she had worn since she was twenty - and opened the door.

"Aunt Rikka!"

The woman who stepped into the room was heavier than Rikka remembered. Her once shining auburn hair had faded to brown. She bore only slight resemblance to the lithe, headstrong girl of long ago. But her eyes were as keen, her gaze as direct, her step as vigorous. She exuded self-confidence.

Marianne has always been strong in body and mind. Rikka forced a smile. "It is good to see you again, Marianne."

The two women clasped hands. Marianne smiled and leaned forward generously as though to embrace the older woman. "Dear Aunt Rikka! Seeing you here brings back old times!"

Rikka stepped back and busied herself taking Marianne's coat, hung it carefully in the small cloak closet, then ushered her into the apartment.

"Now you must sit down here in this poor excuse for a living room and let me serve you coffee."

"Oh, Aunt Rikka, don't you like this apartment? I think Kris has done very well for himself in the years he has been here. You wouldn't want him to waste his money on some expensive place when he can live cheaply here, would you?"

"No, no, of course not." Rikka spoke impatiently. "This place is just fine, with the running water and gas stove and so on and so forth. Very modern. Very convenient."

"Thorstein has made a nice little home for his family, too. You must be so proud of your boys and all they have accomplished."

Marianne spoke warmly and Rikka was reminded that much of "the boys" success was due to Marianne's kindness. But to acknowledge that might lead to uncomfortable depths. Rikka instinctively turned the conversation to safer, shallower waters.

"Yes, it is a cozy house, a fine place for him and Hazel to raise their family. But I have always liked open spaces better than the city. The country life agrees best with me."

Marianne stirred more cream into her coffee and nodded. "Yes, I know. I think it comes from growing up between mountains and sea. Always looking up or looking out. I feel the same way. Never happier than when I can get away from the hospital and the traffic and spend a few days away from it all in the woods."

"The woods!"

"Yes, the woods!" Marianne mimicked her, laughing. "Didn't the boys tell you about my little hideaway? Nurses don't get paid a lot, but I've been saving. Finally bought my own place, a cabin in the woods where I can get away on my holidays, chop wood or pick berries or hike the back trails. Only a half hour by car from the city. You knew I got an automobile, didn't you? Not new, but it's a nice little sedan. Kris and Thorstein have driven out to the cabin with me several times. It's quite a hoot."

No wonder she looks so strong. And brown. And happy. Marianne always did do exactly as she pleased.

Aloud, Rikka only said stiffly, "It sounds very nice."

Silence, as Marianne studied the older woman, her blue eyes unblinking as Rikka sipped her coffee and feigned interest in the pigeons flying past the window.

"But tell me, how are you, Aunt Rikka?"

"Oh, fine, I am fine. Nothing to complain of."

"You never were one for complaining, were you."

Rikka looked up into a gaze as uncompromising as her own. "No, why should one complain? The good Lord knows what we can take and never gives us more than we can bear ..."

"Hogwash! Haven't you ever wanted to scream, 'Stop, I can't take any more?' I know I have!"

They had been speaking only English until this point, but Marianne's outburst was in old country Norwegian.

The pain in Rikka's throat returned, making it impossible to reply. She shook her head.

"But you know what I have learned, Aunt Rikka? It is not really the terrible things that happen to us that are unbearable. It is all the awfulness that we deny, the pain we don't acknowledge. That is what can poison our lives."

"Yes, yes, you are right. No doubt it is our own actions that cause most of our pain. Sin brings consequences." Rikka had found her voice again, insisting by her return to English that old times be spoken of only in generalities. She resumed the polite formal tone she had used when Marianne first entered the apartment.

Marianne smiled a smile as insincere as Rikka's tone and shrugged. The conversation turned to news about mutual acquaintances and friends of the family. Marianne asked after her cousins and half brothers and sisters in Canada, and Rikka gave details of births, deaths, and marriages. Eventually every relationship had been covered. It seemed there was nothing more to say.

Marianne glanced at her watch, exclaimed at the lateness of the afternoon, gathered her handbag and coat, and adjusted her jaunty little hat.

As she went through the doorway, she turned and grasped Rikka's hand.

"It's alright, Aunt Rikka, to be sad. But don't blame yourself. Or me. We all did the best we could at the time."

Shaken, Rikka closed the door behind her sister's daughter. Suddenly the little apartment with its dingy linoleum floor and harsh electric lighting and pervasive odour of gas felt unbearable. With trembling hands, she took her long black coat off the hook by the door and let herself out, remembering just in time to pocket the key before the door locked behind her. She hurried down the stairs and out into dull autumn sunshine. There was a park just a few blocks away, where children played on swings and old men sat on park benches. She could walk those gravel paths as invisible as a ghost. No one there would know her. She could let herself remember.

Remember all the things she could not forget.

Chapter 2

Vikna, 1866

The child flopped down on the rough shingle by the water's edge. In her wild scramble down the cliff, her own angry sobs and the clatter of dislodged stone had hidden the sound of pursuit. Now, as her breathing slowed, she could hear them.

"Rikka, Rikka, come back!"

Her sister's calls were thin and far away. Her brother's voice sounded louder, he must have followed her, maybe seen her heading for the cliff. Rikka rolled out of his line of vision, closer to the cliff face, hoping he had not glimpsed her white pinafore. Maybe he would think she was gone for good, taken by the sea. Like father. Face down on the cold stones, holding her breath, she listened to them shouting her name. She did not move.

As their voices receded, she raised her head and sat with her back against the rock face. The sky was gray and the water a pale gray green, the rocks dark slate. No one at the top of the cliff could see her unless they were to risk their necks peering over the edge into the hollow at the base a hundred feet below. As far as she knew, in all her child's wisdom, no one else in all the island's long history had ever climbed down this cliff as she had just done.

She rolled over on her back and stared up at the sky, feeling at once defiant and fearful. Why did Kristian tease her so? She had really believed that he meant to drown her kitten when he held it over the bridge railing. And then to hear him laughing, "Bare tulla!" Just kidding, just kidding! That had enraged her. Her kitten forgotten, she had flung herself at him, fists and feet flying. Kristine had come running from the house, scolding as though she were their mother, not their thirteen-year-old sister. How could Kristine blame her, Rikka, when it was all Kris' fault? And why did Kristine call her that? A little monster?

The tears rolled down her cheeks and into the corners of her mouth. They tasted salty, like the sea. *Maybe I am a monster. A sea-monster.*

Am I a changeling? How could I know if the fairies brought me? Rikka's breath caught in her throat. Maybe she was only a little girl on her outside, but on the inside was something else. Just now, when she had been so angry, she had felt like a different being, not at all like her Mama's cheerful little girl. She had wanted to hit Kris hard and make him hurt, as much as his teasing hurt her. Maybe she had been switched at birth, by a troll or a mountain spirit, like the ones old Nils told her about. *Maybe the sea monster who brought the storm – the storm that hurled my father into the maelstrom on the very day I was born – maybe it cast a curse on me.*

Maybe I am really a monster.

But, in the stories that Nils the pig keeper and Anna the dairymaid told, monsters always had magical powers. If she were a monster, even a monster who did not know she was one, she should be able to make herself invisible or change herself into a terrifying shape. She would like to be able to do that, to scare Kris and Kristine. She tried it out, muttering some of the magic spells she had heard the pig-keeper mutter when Anna annoyed him. At least, they sounded to her like magic spells. But when she had tried to tell Kristine about them, Kristine had stopped her, saying "Rikka, don't repeat Nils' bad words. Mama would wash your mouth out with soap if she heard you!"

Even now, all alone on this silent beach, she did not quite dare say the words aloud, but only whispered one or two. A cold breeze sprang up, sending little ripples lapping at the waters' edge in front of her. It sent a chill through her as well. What if they were magic words? calling up a monster to take her deep under the waves? to take her family away?

She sprang to her feet and trotted down the beach. The clouds lifted from the western horizon and shafts of late afternoon sunshine gleamed on wet rocks. The incoming tide might catch her if the monsters did not. It was a long way home to go around by the shore path. But even she, brave Rikka, the only person (so far as she knew) ever to climb down the sheer rock face on the island of Vest Vikna, even she would not risk climbing back up that cliff. She only wanted to get home, cuddle her kitten, and be assured that Kristine and Kris and dear Mama were not hurt by her evil magic words. She would likely get a thrashing for fighting with Kris and running away from Kristine, but that would be nothing like as bad as the pain of thinking that she may have hurt them.

Deep inside, she knew they loved her and wished her well.

Even if she were a monster.

But Rikka never did get that thrashing. Her fears were forgotten almost as soon as she ran in the door. Kristine had astutely guessed that Kristian had again been teasing Rikka and she lectured him on his duty as the elder of the two to set a good example for his little sister.

Mortified at Kristine's scolding, Kris ran off to join his friends and forgot about Rikka. Kristine returned to the house and her task of help sweeping out the big work room where her mother and a few other women sat spinning wool. When Rikka slipped through the door, Mama scarcely looked up from her spinning wheel.

"Rikka, how do you get so dirty?" she scolded. "Go wash your hands and change your apron. "

Then she picked up the thread of her conversation with Kristine as though there had been no interruption.

"Yes, it is best that we plan to do this now. You have finished your years at the folkeskole, and there is no one here who can teach you more. The young man Pastor Olsen recommends will tutor you besides giving music lessons."

Rikka stopped short.

"Mama! Kristine gets her own tutor? All to herself? Can't I have one too?"

Marie laughed and shook her head. "Rikka, Rikka, a tutor is not a kitten or a puppy, I cannot get one for each of you! You will of course go to the folkeskole, as all the children do, and learn to read and write and cipher. If young Mr. Arnold has time, he will help you and Kris and the other youngsters at the school with your music. Maybe you will have a concert for the Christmas eve service at the church."

* * *

Mr. Arnold arrived the next week from Rorvik, brought by their ship's captain, Edvard Brevig. Edvard had been Rikka's idol until this point, tall and brown and, she believed, brave. He must be brave, as he sailed her mother's fishing schooner to the most dangerous parts of creation, the wild cold sea and rock-strewn coastal waters where sea serpents or kraken like the one who took her father might still lurk. Rikka hoped that Edvard never guessed how completely he tumbled from first place in her world when young Mr. Arnold walked ashore. But since he had never guessed his hero status, the loss was no loss at all to him.

Mr. Arnold, with his laughing eyes and quick wit, was given an upstairs room in the men's house where the farm labourers stayed and where Captain Edvard kept his extra gear and slept while in port. As was customary, they all ate together in the big kitchen/dining hall adjoining Marie's work room, hearty meals and well prepared if lacking in variety. Rikka managed to wiggle onto the chair next to Arnold at his first supper at their house and kept to that place so consistently that no one thought of her sitting anywhere else at the big plank table.

Although everyone took an immediate liking to Arnold, Rikka was the one who openly adored him. The day after his arrival, he visited the folkeskole and the old school master proposed a schedule for music lessons to be included at the end of the regular school day. Those afternoons became the high points of Rikka's week. When they walked back to the house together from the little village school, she engaged all his attention with her chatter, as Kristian usually dashed off to join his friends on some boyish adventure before he was expected home.

But once at home, it was plain to all that Arnold had eyes only for Kristine. Kristine, with her red-gold hair and pure complexion, her perfect manners and quiet dignity that seemed so much older than her years.

Rikka saw it too. It seemed there was to be no one in all the world who preferred her above all others. Her kittens did, she reminded herself, and Mama, when asked one night whom she loved best, had said, "I love you best as my little girl, and Kristian best as my big boy, and Kristine best as my big girl." Not really satisfying. Especially as it came after a reminder that the scripturally correct answer was, "Of course I love my Saviour best, and so should you."

Much as it hurt, it could be no surprise to her that Mr. Arnold preferred her sister's company over hers. Kristine was the one whom he tutored in geography and literature and arithmetic as well as music, the one he talked with as though she were almost a grown-up lady. But more than that, Kristine was simply perfect. Rikka, most definitely, was not.

Oftentimes she felt hurt and angry - feelings she was determined to keep to herself, ashamed to be found out. Rikka knew what the catechism had to say about jealousy. Coveting anything that belonged to another was a sin. But sometimes the effort of stifling those angry jealous thoughts hurt so much she wanted to cry. She discovered a secret trick of staving off angry tears by grinning fiercely, which seemed somehow to stop tears forming. Her reward for this was Kristian hooting about "Rikka's ugly smile."

But as the lessons progressed, she had one consolation. Because she gave such complete and utter attention to her beloved teacher, her music progressed at a great rate. By Christmas she had a solo piece in the concert, and even old Nils the pig-herd scrubbed his face and put on a clean shirt to come and hear her play. She felt as though all her sorrow, all her despair at being the youngest and least of the family melted away and for a few precious minutes the music lifted her to royal standing. She became for that moment the first and the best.

Her Mama even began talking about possibly sending to Trondheim for a piano of their own, so that Henrikka could practise at home.

Rikka vowed to work hard at her music and become the best.

Then Mr. Arnold and everyone else would love her.

Chapter 3

West Vikna, 1872

"And at Kristiansund, we will take the steamship for Kristiania."

Rikka squealed with excitement and bounced so hard the old three-legged stool tipped her over onto the kitchen floor. She landed hard on her bottom, arms straight up, still holding the wooden bowl full of bright red berries. Her mother laughed aloud and shook her head in mock despair at Rikka. Sigrid clucked in annoyance and left her butter churn for a moment to retrieve the bowl and set it safely on the table. Rikka scrambled to her feet.

"Mama, I promise, I will work so hard, you will be proud of me!"

Six years have passed - six years in which Rikka has grown to be almost as tall as Kristine, almost a young lady. Almost, but not quite. Rikka saw in her mother's eyes the amused look she often turned on her younger daughter. She could almost hear her mother's thoughts, sometimes expressed in an exasperated sigh or gentle reproof. Rikka, be careful. Pay attention. Sit still.

And the unspoken admonition: Try to be more like Kristine.

Her mother sat across from her at the table where they had been picking twigs, leaves and the occasional bug from the berries Rikka and Kristian had gathered earlier this morning. The berry rake still hung by the open door, but Kristian had conveniently disappeared on another adventure when their mother exclaimed over the debris they had gathered with the berries.

Marie smiled, but said in a reproving tone, "Of course I will expect you to work hard, and to act like a well brought up young lady. You must remember that in Kristiania, you will be judged as you behave. No bouncing, no squealing or tumbling on the floor like a child!"

Late summer sunshine poured through the open doorway. The sweet spicy smell of lingenberry pie baking in the oven filled the room. Rikka resumed her task, carefully sifting the berries through her fingers and dropping them onto a tray that would go on the drying rack. The day had been perfect so far and now it was capped by this news, so wonderful Rikka scarcely dared believe it. After weeks of uncertainty, it was finally decided: Rikka, her mother and Kristian were to spend the winter in Kristiania.

Pastor Olsen had entered Rikka in a regional piano competition the previous May. Rikka's age barely qualified, her birthday coming only a week before the event in Trondheim. But, to the astonishment of everyone except herself, the pastor and Mr. Arnold, her performance had won top marks for her age group against children two or three years older. And the prize? Music lessons in Kristiania, at a school sponsored by none other than the Queen herself!

Before their astonishment entirely died down, Marie had decided that out of necessity the scholarship must be declined.

"Rikka is far too young to go from home without me. And how can I possibly leave the island? Who will take care of the farm, our business, our home? To move my family halfway across the country for the sake of music lessons! Impossible!"

But then the letter arrived.

Pastor Olsen had told his elderly aunt, who lived in Kristiania, about the talented young musician in his congregation.

"Having heard from my dear nephew, Fredrik Olsen, about your daughter," the old woman wrote, "it pleases me to offer my assistance. I live alone. My house is large and empty. If you and your children can leave your home in Vikna for the winter months while the school is in session, you would be most welcome to share my home with me while your daughter attends music school."

"I see this as a clear sign that we should go to Kristiania," her mother conceded. "God must want you to continue your music, Rikka-girl."

"It almost seems foreordained," Marie remarked to Sigrid, who was her friend and confidante as well as the person who oversaw everyday household chores. It was Sigrid who whipped up piecrust and ordered Rikka to roll it out, fit it in the pan and fill it with berries, then top it with another thin rich crust. In this home, as in most others on these coastal islands, roles were so blurred as to be inconsequential in daily life. All worked together and ate together. The unmarried workers lived with the family. Sigrid, who had not married and had no intention of doing so, would stay with them forever, Rikka knew.

"If you want to eat, you must learn there is more to lingenberry pie than just picking the berries," Sigrid had told her sternly. Rikka knew that any of the serving women could have made the pie, but it pleased her to know that she, Rikka, would be credited with the first lingenberry pie of the season.

Marie continued in a musing tone, speaking to herself as much as to Sigrid.

"A year ago, I would not have dreamed of leaving Kristine in charge here." Sigrid glanced at her with the hint of a scowl on her usually impassive face, and Marie quickly amended that statement.

"Oh, of course, you, Sigrid, will continue to see everything is done in good order. Kristine will benefit from your wisdom, while getting some practical experience managing a house. She will depend on you even more than I do. Her hands will be quite full, teaching the little scholars at the folkeskole. No, I meant something else entirely … you know, if Arnold were still living here, it would have been awkward. You know what I mean."

There had been many changes in recent months. After four years of tutoring first Kristine and then Kristian, as well as teaching music at the folkeskole, Mr. Arnold had announced it was time for a change. He joined Captain Edvard's crew aboard the old fishing schooner to sail up the coast to the Lofoten Islands, chasing after the schools of herring and cod. Kristine had for the past several months assisted the elderly school master of the folkeskole, teaching the primary pupils. The old man declared he was more than ready to retire and, much to Marie's surprise, suggested to the local parish board that Kristine take over his role.

The Norwegian board of examiners, after much letter writing and requests for proof of her penmanship and general competency in history and mathematics, reluctantly agreed to approve Kristine's certificate. The parish hired her as teacher forthwith.

Rikka, lost in her own happy thoughts as she mechanically continued cleaning the mounds of berries, resurfaced at the mention of Mr. Arnold. She had long ago accepted the fact that Arnold and Kristine were meant for each other, and she delighted in their not-so-secret romance. Only her mother had seemed oblivious to it, perhaps blinded by Kristine's calm manner and Arnold's habitual playfulness.

"He is a good man, but … I mean to say, Kristine is so young, still just a girl."

But now, thought Rikka, Kristine will be a grownup woman with her own income from the school.

The following weeks sped by as preparations were made for Rikka, Kristian and their mother to leave for Kristiania.

Kristian, at fifteen, was eager to leave childhood and school behind him and had protested vigorously that he did not want to "be dragged along behind Mama and Rikka just when all the other fellows are finally getting to have some fun." Several of his classmates intended to sign on as crew for the fishing fleet. Kris had already broached his plan to Captain Brevig.

"Mama, lots of fishermen went to sea when they were no older than I am. Edvard said he would sign me up if you would only give him the go-ahead - and Arnold will be on the same crew. What could go wrong?"

But his mother was firm. She had other plans for him. After a flurry of letters to friends and acquaintances in Kristiania, she found two options she approved. He had his choice: he could apprentice with a merchant, or a shipbuilder. Kris sulked and kicked the cat and refused to look at his mother when she pointed out that he would need skills in a trade or commerce to step into his pre-ordained role as overseer of the family business.

In the end, Rikka's excitement infected him too, and he generously promised his envious friends that they could join him when he returned to start his own ship-building business.

Peder, the farm manager, offered to take over the management of their general store as well as the farm, because he and his wife already did most of the ordering for Marie. Her absolute trust in Peder's integrity and his wife's shrewdness made it easy for Marie to acquiesce to this suggestion. For the next few years, the day-by-day management of her business would be entrusted to their capable hands.

With all the world seeming to be in flux, Kristine and Arnold felt there was no longer any reason to delay. The young couple declared their engagement.

Marie consented. Although the more unsympathetic members of the community thought Arnold too light-hearted, a cheerful heart was no drawback to someone embarking on a career that demanded optimism as well as hardiness. Everyone knew that he was as likely as any other young fisherman to succeed. With his share of the season's catch secured, there was nothing to prevent these two from marrying in the spring. Marie only stipulated they wait until she, Kris and Rikka returned from Kristiania.

Plans were made, goodbyes said, clothes mended, wool sweaters and socks knit by every pair of female hands in the busy household. Anna would take charge of the dairy, the half-dozen serving women and farm workers would continue their occupations as usual. Sigrid and Pastor Olsen's wife promised to keep a close eye on Kristine.

Rikka's thoughts were miles and months away. "Mama! The King and Queen live in Kristiania, don't they?"

"Yes, Rikka, they sometimes live there. When not at home in Sweden."

Rikka smiled her secretive little smile. She would not divulge her dream to Mother's kind indulgence, and certainly not to her brother's ridicule. Maybe, just maybe, if she worked very hard and memorized everything her teachers told her - maybe someday she would play for the Queen.

Chapter 4

Vikna, 1875

The ship sailed through the rock-bound channel between the islands, its sails snapping in the breeze. That familiar sound and the harsh scream of gulls brought a smile to Rikka's lips. She pulled her heavy coat tighter around her shoulders and squinted into the glare of reflected sunlight. She should be able to see their warehouse by now, its whiteness standing out in sharp contrast to the black and gray of the rocks. There! A glint from one of the tall windows, shining golden in the sun, caught her eye.

We are almost home.

Even after living for most of three years in Kristiania, it had never really felt like home. She tried her best to hide her homesickness, ashamed and surprised at the strange sadness she felt. The day she had first sailed away from Vikna with Mama and Kristian, she had thought herself the luckiest girl alive.

Since Kristine and Arnold's marriage, Rikka discovered she did not miss her sister as much as she had expected. Their relationship, always unequal, had lost a closeness that Rikka had taken for granted without being aware of it. Kristine belongs to Mr. Arnold now. *And I – well, I guess I belong to my music!*

Most of all, it was the entire experience of being at home that Rikka missed. Sometimes such longing came over her that she gave up and dissolved into tears. Mama found her red-eyed and sobbing, crumpled under her rough wool blankets.

"It is natural," Mama said, "for you to miss living in a house of our own. Heaven knows I do, too!"

Mrs. Olsen had asked them to think of her home as their own, indeed had insisted so often they not 'stand on ceremony' that it had quite the opposite effect. It was very much Mrs. Olsen's house, her furniture, her fussily perfect hardanger embroidery that decorated every level surface. The poor old lady was so intensely grateful for the supplies Marie bought, and the help Marie provided with housekeeping, that Rikka wondered cattily how the old lady could have kept body and soul together without the benefit of their presence.

Now Rikka watched the familiar buildings taking shape in the distance, tiny pale beads that gradually solidified into rectangles. *No. It was not our house I missed. It was this whole island, the sharp smell of sea air, the gleam of sunlight on wet rocks, that feeling of being known by everyone and everything. The rocks remember me, the gulls are spreading the news. I am back. I am home.*

Through all their months in Kristiania, that vague restless unhappiness had left her only in the hours she spent practising her piano or studying for the next lesson. Lost in a world of chords and harmonies, the gray sadness that tugged at her like a subtle undertow melted away. She would find herself instead soaring into jubilation.

Rikka sometimes wondered whether she would ever again be the ordinary unselfconscious girl she had been before they went to Kristiania, before she became a woman. The two events seemed to her inextricably linked.

Her monthly flow had started last year. Discreet as her mother and Mrs. Olsen had been, Kristian had divined her alarm, and the reason for it. Thereafter, he provoked her by insinuating that girls were, after all, not good for much of anything but tears and tantrums after a certain age, until they finally married and settled down to having babies, as Kristine was doing. Her flushed cheeks and angry retorts seemed only to prove his point. Maybe he could not resist teasing her, any more than she could stop herself from reacting. She wondered whether he truly believed what he said.

Rikka realized it was a common view among men, this belittling attitude towards females, and she wondered fearfully if they were right, if her extremes of joy and sadness were nothing more than the ridiculous fate of all girls helplessly doomed to become women.

That thought frightened her and she set it aside. *Nothing is inevitable. I have two things that make me happy – Vikna and music. I will cling to both. I will never again drown in sadness.* Thrilled as she was to be returning home, she worried her music would stagnate. How could she hope to progress without anyone to teach her? She had so much yet to learn! She promised herself again, as she did almost every day, that she would continue to practise and strive to be the best she could be, even without a teacher to help her.

She had attended concerts and recitals in Kristiania, initially with her mother, Kristian and Mrs. Olsen, later with her fellow students and her teachers. From the first time she heard the compositions of Beethoven and Greig she had hungered to play their music. The heavy magnificence of Handel, the sweetness of Chopin, melted her bones and made her spirit soar. When she was invited to join a group of students chosen to perform a concert for their patron, the Queen, she was excited but not alarmed. She knew she could do justice to the beauty of the music.

Queen Sophia, despite the flamboyant red velvet and sparkling jewels she wore, had a quiet look and appeared a thoughtful, attentive listener. Rikka could feel the Queen's eyes fixed on her as she played the difficult selections her teacher had chosen. She glanced up as she rose from her curtsy and for a moment their eyes met. Rikka smiled. The Queen smiled back and nodded, as though to say, "Well done." Rikka would never forget that moment.

Kristine had written to her. "Dear sister, we congratulate you on your success. You should be proud to have played before the Queen. But I do hope you will not let it go to your head and that you are not expecting too much from your music. We miss you and I know Mama is happy to be back home."

Marie had returned to the island a few months earlier to help Kristine. Two babies in less than two years! Kristine and Arnold had wasted no time once they were safely married.

Hidden between the lines of neatly penned script, Rikka discerned another message. *Mother has grandchildren now.* Kristine and Arnold, still living in her mother's home, needed a house and farm to support their growing family. Why should her mother siphon off the family's resources to support Rikka's impractical dream of becoming a concert pianist?

In her calm, reasonable manner, Kristine had given Rikka to understand it would be a waste of time and money for her to continue to strive for anything more than casual proficiency. If she could play well enough for church services, weddings, and funerals, what more did she want?

Rikka felt a familiar resentment well up in her soul. Kristine was so sure she knew best, for herself and her family. But Rikka wanted more.

She stretched her fingers out in the cold morning sunshine and looked at them critically. Her hands were large, long fingered, and strong. "Peasant's hands," one teacher had said.

"No," another had corrected him, "Artist's hands. It takes strength of mind and body to play strong music. The spirit needs muscle!"

Rikka had liked that. She never felt ashamed of her physical self, and certainly not of her hands. *The spirit needs muscle.*

Since that September morning when they had left Vikna, she had returned to the island for only a few weeks each summer. Kristian had perhaps missed home as much as she had, though for different reasons, and more impatiently. His longing for the sea only grew stronger during the brief apprenticeship his mother had insisted he serve with a merchant in the city's bustling warehouse district.

"You will be in charge of our business someday," his mother explained.

But the merchant finally declared, "Take the boy! He has no interest in business!" Kris' mother relented and agreed that he try the second option she had offered him. If not a life at sea, at least an apprenticeship with a shipwright was heading him in the direction he wanted to go. Someday he could build his own sailing ship.

"We could sail all the way to America," he told Rikka.

* * *

Kristian had been chatting with some of the crew and now joined Rikka at the ship's rail. "Won't it be great to be home, doing something useful? I will never live in the city again, not as long as I live. I might never leave Vikna again."

Rikka laughed at him.

"So, you have already given up your great plan? Not sailing to America?"

"All in good time, little sister, all in good time. I wrote to Brevig, told him I wanted to join his crew. By the time I turn twenty, I will have my own ship, my own crew, be a captain myself. I know exactly what kind of ship I want to build."

36

"Good for you." Rikka beamed at her sturdy ruddy-faced brother. She felt a surge of affection for this exasperating but always interesting boy. *Not boy. He is a Man now,* she reminded herself. *He's a man and can make his own decisions. Whereas I – what can I do?* She turned her back to him and gazed towards their island home. Her brother was going to begin the life he planned for himself, but her plans could never be anything but dreams without the support of her family. *Why should it be so much harder for a girl to do what she wants to do, and make her living doing it?*

I will find some way to use my music, she promised herself. *I will plan my own life.*

That turned out to be even more difficult than she had expected. Some plans had been already made for her.

Her mother and Kristine were at the dock to meet them. They had brought with them Kristine's little daughter, Marianne. She gazed curiously at Rikka from the security of her grandmother's arms. Her wide blue eyes brightened at the sight of Kris, as though she already recognized him as a friend, and when he tickled her chin and offered her a sweet, she smiled and held out her arms for a cuddle. Kristine embraced first him and then Rikka, exclaiming that they both seemed bigger. Rikka knew very well that her height had not changed, she had not grown an inch in the last year. For a moment she wondered uneasily if Kristine meant that she looked fat but put that thought out of her mind as she recalled the sight of her own slim upright image in the stateroom mirror that morning. *I do look more grown up, now that I have a bosom!*

After two children, Kristine's figure was a little fuller but to Rikka's eyes she was as beautiful as ever, her hair glossy smooth, her face serene, her smile welcoming. She slipped her arm through Rikka's.

"Mama and I have the most wonderful welcome home supper planned for you tonight. Just our own household, we have so much to talk about! And Mama has promised Pastor Olsen that you will teach music lessons to the children at the folkeskole. Everyone is looking forward to hearing you play for church next Sunday, too."

Rikka didn't know what to say. *At least I will get to use my music.*

They walked a little ahead of Marie and Kris, who, with the little girl between them, made slow progress up the steep path. Rikka noticed Kristine's complexion had a translucent lustre and she recalled that her mother had returned to the island because of her concern over Kristine's health.

"Are you feeling better now, Kristine? Mama wrote that you were ill, and she was glad she had gone home to look after you."

Kristine squeezed her arm. "Nothing to worry about, sister dear. I just needed a little rest. Having a second baby so soon after our first took the wind out of my sails for a time. And now with another on the way …"

"What? Another baby? You're pregnant again?" Rikka whirled about to face Kristine.

Kristine laughed and patted her cheek as though she were a child. "Is that so surprising? I thought you knew that was why Mama came home to help me. Those first months, the nausea, can be awful. You will understand some day."

It astonished and annoyed Rikka to discover herself still trapped in the role of younger sister. She wondered whether it was always going to be this way, her mother and sister assuming she was too naïve or immature to be privy to grownup concerns. *I must prove to them I am no longer just a girl!*

In the next weeks her resolve hardened. Her mother and Kristian had conversations that became progressively shorter and louder and finally culminated with Kristian shouting, "Mama, for the last time, I am not going to be a storekeeper!" and slamming the door as he left the house

No one ever slammed doors in Marie's house.

Kristian moved his gear over to the men's house and took to spending every day with Captain Brevig's crew as they prepared the fishing gear, dories, and schooner for the next fishing trip. Mealtime conversation gradually included tacit acknowledgement of his new role as a fisherman, one of the crew.

Amid all this drama, Arnold and Kristine were preoccupied with building their house. Babies, building, store, school - there were disruptions enough to provide Rikka with opportunities to demonstrate her willingness to help. She redoubled her efforts, determined to make herself useful. Did they notice? She doubted that any of them, absorbed as they were in their own concerns, saw half of what she did.

With Kristian at least temporarily settled on his own path, it seemed the time was ripe for her to assert herself. After all, her mother had often said that a family business rested upon the character of the family. Their store had been managed by her mother ever since her father's death, continuing to supply West Vikna and the schooners heading up the coast to the Lofoten Island fishing ground. A reputation earned over generations might be lost if continuity were disrupted. Rikka sympathized with her mother's reluctance to continue shouldering the whole burden of business. Who knew how many years it might be until her son or son-in-law grew out of their infatuation with the sea? Arnold promised Kristine that he would build up their farm to a point where it would become his main occupation, but Rikka privately doubted that day would ever come. He so obviously loved his time away at sea, relished being one of a crew of men setting off for the wild blue islands. Even after they returned home, he never tired of long evenings drinking and swapping stories about their adventures. How could the settled life of a farmer or storekeeper compare to that, Rikka wondered?

As for Kristian – well, Rikka thought that her mother would be a very, very old lady before he changed his mind.

It seemed that Marie thought the same. "Really, all I want to do right now is to be marmar to these little ones," her mother said, squeezing baby Arvor's chubby cheeks until he giggled. "Wonderful as it was to have Peder and Hanne take over managing the store while I was in Kristiania, now that I am home, they are glad to have only the farm to worry about. That is as it should be, everyone doing their own work and all of us helping each other when needed. But maybe I need to bring in new blood. Someone young and strong to learn the business and take over for me."

An able young man must be trained to take over her business, at least until Kristian was ready to "listen to reason", as she put it.

One afternoon as her mother sat at the worktable in the office at the back of the store frowning at the big ledger spread before her, Rikka approached her.

"Mama, you have so much work to do. Let me help."

"I can help you," she repeated as her mother looked up, surprised. "I want to manage the store for you."

Marie smiled at her. "That is sweet of you, dear. When I hire a young man to take over, maybe you can help him with ordering or stocking supplies…"

"But why does it have to be a man?" Rikka could hear the childish petulance in her own voice and forced herself to stop and take a few deep breaths, calming herself as her teacher had taught her to do before a recital. "I am as smart as Kristian. In school, I was better than him in arithmetic and almost everything else. I am old enough – why, some girls are already married at my age. I am fourteen. If I were a boy, I could apprentice or go to sea. Why won't you let me try? You have always managed everything by yourself. If you will teach me, I know I can learn!"

"Rikka, you don't know what you are asking. It is not a suitable occupation for a young girl. I had no choice, I had to take over management when your father died. You have no idea how hard it was, with you an infant and Kristine and Kristian so small. I had to sink or swim. You are a brave and clever girl, and I am proud that you want to help. But it is out of the question."

Her mother patted Rikka's smooth brown braids and told her she would have quite enough to do, teaching music lessons.

Then her mother, predictably, asked their pastor's advice.

Pastor Olsen said he knew a young fellow in Trondheim, the son of a missionary-school teacher, who might be just the man for the job. Marie hired the young man sight unseen.

Months passed and Rikka slipped into the role the whole community seemed to expect of her. She was always available to help Kristine or Sigrid or her mother. She taught music lessons to the children, played for church services when required - the elderly organist was not quite ready to relinquish his place to this slip of a girl, even though she had played for the Queen - and found that life was, on the whole, very good. But like a stone in her shoe, there was a constant irritation. That stone was called Mentz.

It had been hard enough to accept her mother's decision to bypass Rikka's sincere offer to learn the family business. Seeing a stranger with no better qualifications than her own given that opportunity was too much to swallow.

Before the interloper arrived, with his letters of introduction from his father, his pastor, and his former employer in Trondheim, Rikka decided she hated him. Then she corrected herself. *Hate is a sin. As a good Christian, I will not hate him, I will just pretend he does not exist.*

That had become increasingly difficult to do, for the well-thought-of young man from Trondheim hardly spoke a dozen words to Rikka in as many months. *How can you ignore someone who does not seem to notice you are walking down the same path, entering the same room, seated across the dinner table from him?*

Sometimes she tried to invent reasons for this. She told herself that he had his own work, his own routine, his own friends. And she had hers. It was natural. They had nothing in common except proximity.

But that didn't wash, as most of her friends soon became his as well. Mentz ate his meals at her mother's table, shared living space with her own brother. Why, then, did she always see him as though from a distance? If she entered a room, Mentz was just leaving. How did that happen? If Rikka came early to a gathering, Mentz arrived late.

What was even worse, she could not attribute this to boyish shyness. He seemed perfectly at ease with other girls. She could name several young ladies only slightly older than herself who shamelessly vied for his attention. Flirted, even. And he seemed to enjoy it.

All in all, Mentz gave every indication to Rikka that she interested him less than any other girl on the island.

It might have been humiliating if Rikka had not been so openly hostile to his arrival and strove to ignore his presence.

Who could have guessed that this paragon, this son of a missionary, this interloper, would bring something every young person on the island needed? Within a month of his arrival, a new sport took the island by storm.

"All the fellows play basse in Trondheim," Mentz remarked at supper one evening. "I brought a ball with me, hoping I might have a game here."

Kristian was enthusiastic. "I've heard about it, but never got to try it myself. It takes some skill, doesn't it! I wonder - how much space would we need to mark out the circles? There is that level field between the schoolhouse and the church that might be just about right..."

Before the evening was over, a group of boys and men had paced off the field. The first game was played a few nights later. It became a meeting place for the young and young-at-heart every fine evening thereafter until snow fell. For boys who felt the need to kick something, it was sheer joy. For girls hoping to be noticed, basse arrived as a heaven-sent gift.

"I don't see the purpose of the game," Rikka said to Kristian, with a disdainful toss of her head. "You don't even have teams or choose sides!"

Kristian laughed and tugged at her braid, loosening a strand from its neat coil. "Don't you see? That's the beauty of it, it's every man for himself. You draw your circle and defend it against the others. If the ball lands in your circle, it counts as a point against you. Three and you're out. The last man standing wins."

"Well, I think it is a silly game," she declared. But how could she stay away when all her friends were there? And how could she help but be aware of the one who threw himself with wholehearted joy into the game, who played with such speed and agility? She might pretend to ignore the young man from Trondheim, but her eyes were continually drawn to him. Although he was neither the biggest nor the strongest, he was without doubt the champion. What a blessed relief it was to stand at the edge of the field with a dozen other girls and cheer and shout and laugh and be quite sure that no one knew it was Mentz, not her brother, not her brother-in-law, nor anyone else, but only Mentz she watched.

To her annoyance, Rikka found that, try as she might, nowhere could she totally ignore Mentz. When he came in the door, he seemed to fill the room. She found herself picking his voice out of a crowd. She noticed his Romanesque nose and his thick straight eyebrows like raven-wings almost meeting over clear blue eyes - eyes that saw everyone but her.

Rikka overheard her mother remark to a friend, "Mentz is good for business." Rikka knew she did not mean only that he was quick to learn the rules and customs of the business, but that customers felt confident their own interests would be protected as well as his employer's.

Although Marie had expressed private doubts about hiring someone so young, in the end she was satisfied she had made the right decision. Customers who might easily have gone elsewhere sailed into the rock-strewn cove of Vikna and anchored by the store perched just above the high waterline. It seemed everyone was happy with this new blood, this addition to their community, this young man called Mentz.

Everyone, that is, but Rikka.

Chapter 5

Vikna, 1876

"Mama, where are those pretty ribbons you saved for me? I want to wear them tonight."

Rikka stamped the snow from her feet and flung her coat on the hook by the door. Her cheeks glowed almost as red as her mittened hands. Her mind swirled with a multitude of things that might ruin this evening's concert.

But as she inhaled the spicy sweet aroma of stewing fruit, her childhood delight in Christmas drove out more grownup concerns.

"Mama, you are making the sot-sup! Did the dried fruit shipment finally arrive? Oh, I hope every house on the island smells this good by tomorrow night!"

Her mother beamed at her. Like Rikka, Christmas was Marie's favourite time of year. She began planning next year's celebration almost the same moment she blew out the candles on this year's Christmas tree. A delay in the shipment of raisins, prunes and dried apples caused consternation in every household on the island but most of all in Marie's.

"Yes, Astrid has a big pot simmering on the stove. We finished the krumkake and julekake this afternoon. There are stacks of flatbrod and lefse stored in the pantry. We will have a wonderful Christmas feast."

She gave her daughter a quick hug. "You are doing your part, too, with the program you've planned for tonight. The children must be so excited."

Rikka made a wry face. "I just hope they remember their parts, and don't freeze-up when they see all eyes on them."

She helped herself to a crisp cookie from the plate of less-than-perfect krumkake, set out as always to be eaten fresh while the best ones were stored away for Christmas Eve.

"Some of them want to bellow as loud as they can, as though it's a cow-calling competition. The shyest ones will forget to sing altogether. But the Antonsen boys' violin duet - just wait 'til you hear them, Mama. I don't think Vikna has ever heard anything so good."

Marie smiled at her daughter and handed her the ribbons she had retrieved from a cupboard drawer.

"Go and get ready, my dear. Everyone will enjoy this concert. There will be no music critics, only parents and grandparents."

And everyone else, thought Rikka as she ran upstairs. *Even Mentz will be there.*

After all, even the young gentleman from Trondheim would be expected to attend the most important community event of the winter.

If only he would pay her some attention. Another year had done nothing to bring them together. They seemed locked in a pattern of mutual avoidance. Rikka's thoughts followed a familiar path. *Why does he never talk to me? When other boys showed up at our door all summer long, asking me to go sailing, or offering to help me with the berry-picking, or wanting to walk with me home from church, Mentz didn't even notice. But of course, I don't care, I have no time to waste on him or any other silly boy. Not with all the island's children clambering for music lessons - and all the preparations for this Christmas program.*

Kristine had warned her that her curt rejection of young men seeking her favour might earn her a reputation as a vain, proud girl. In this tight-knit community, being known as standoffish was a reputation hard to live down. Rikka scoffed.

Now, dressed in her best dress, her hair brushed and with the pretty new ribbons entwined in the gleaming braid encircling her brow, she deliberately refrained from bursting into an unladylike trot as she hurried back over the well-trodden path through the snow to the schoolhouse. This concert would show everyone on the island that she, Henrikka Arntsdatter Lund, was not proud or vain, but a modest, hard-working teacher. Tonight, she would show only a gracious demeanor. The island mothers would, she hoped, be proud of their children's efforts. If this concert confirmed her as an accomplished teacher as well as first-rate musician, they would claim her triumph as their own.

Rikka had absorbed a basic tenet of village life: expending time and money on a skill that did not clearly benefit everyone was nothing more than sinful individualism. On the other hand, making good music was valued as something they could all enjoy.

She was eager to show off the progress some of her students had made. *Take the Antonsen boys, for example.* When Andreas Antonsen had mentioned shyly one day early in the fall that his two eldest boys, shaggy headed ten- and eleven-year-olds, had taught themselves to play a little on his violin and now hoped the new teacher would give them lessons, Rikka had listened with a sinking heart. She had studied piano and organ; her knowledge of other instruments was rudimentary at best. But, as her mother pointed out that evening as they sat by the fireplace, she could do the children no harm by teaching them what she did know. Maybe she would learn more herself as her pupils progressed.

It was true. Practising the correct technique of holding the bow, experiencing the difference each small adjustment made to the sound they drew forth from the instrument, was a revelation to the boys and to Rikka. Shy Parelius and grinning Anton looked upon Rikka as nothing short of divine in her wisdom and ability. While Rikka knew full well their success owed more to their faithful perseverance than to her ability, the admiration they bestowed on her increased her confidence. She introduced them to a few of her favorite pieces, difficult compositions when compared to the simple folk melodies they had played by ear. The music spoke to them as it had spoken to her. Teacher and pupil were drawn closer by this shared enjoyment. She hoped the same would be true of their parents, grandparents, and neighbours.

She brushed the snow from the steps and opened the schoolhouse door.

Anton and Parelius were the first of the students to arrive. While Rikka lit the lamps she told them they must be her ushers, greet the audience and help with chairs and so on. She could feel their excitement and knew she must keep their restless limbs and nervous minds occupied. Somehow calming them calmed her. She felt energized and confident. As the children and their families arrived, first a trickle and then a flood, filling the schoolhouse wall to wall, she knew beyond any doubt that this would be an evening she would always remember.

* * *

The smaller children, acutely aware that they had the attention of not only their mothers but the entire community, hardly blinked as they lined up with eyes focused on Rikka. They sang as they had never sung before. When it came Anton's turn, and his trembling bow brought forth a disastrous shriek from his violin, Rikka feared that he would run from the stage in tears. But she smiled at him encouragingly and stopped playing the piano accompaniment until he indicated with a nod that he was ready to start over. The second time he came in softly, delicately, and the music soared to its grand conclusion. Every mother and grandmother in the audience had suffered with him and his success became everyone's success. The applause rattled the windows. The rest of the children performed their pieces admirably and without incident. Rikka played one modern composition by Grieg,

53

then moved into a medley of traditional Christmas music. The audience joined the school children singing old favourites, harmonizing effortlessly. The pastor's closing prayer was brief and cheerful. Then the congratulations began.

The winter moon cast its glow over the wide snowy yard as the door was flung open and lamplight spilled out. The first to leave were the very old, wrapped in shawls and smiles, shaking hands with the young music instructor as they went out the door. Amidst the confusion of voices and laughter could be heard frequent compliments.

"Such lovely music ... thank you, my dear ... I had no idea that Jon could sing like that ... when did Anton learn to play the violin?"

Rikka stood in the cold draft by the door, splendid in her long dark skirt and brightly embroidered apron, her brown braid shining, the satin ribbons gleaming scarlet. Her eyes shone as she responded to the well-wishers.

"Thank you, good night, gud nacht, gud jule to all of you and your family, yes, see you tomorrow at Christmas Eve service!"

* * *

When the last straggler had gone, and come back again to find a lost mitten, and the door closed behind him, Rikka sank to the floor laughing. She looked up at Kristine, who had stayed behind to help her tidy up. "Oh, what an evening, what a night! Wasn't it fun, though? Even the mishaps were perfect, everyone enjoyed seeing the little ones so entranced by the tree and the swinging lamps that they just stood and stared for a moment and then began waving at their parents … oh I will never forget it!"

The door burst open again, but this time, instead of a bonneted mama or red-cheeked child returning with more thanks or felicitations, two robust smiling young men entered. Arnold and Mentz stamped the snow off their boots as Arnold said, "We saw the crowd leave and thought you ladies could use a hand straightening up the place."

"Why thank you, kind sir!" Kristine smiled sweetly at her husband. "Don't imagine I failed to see you slip out while Mama and I were getting the children bundled up. It looked as though you planned to escape your family for the rest of the evening. As you so often do."

Although what Kristine said was, in fact, quite true of Arnold's behaviour in recent months, and her tone was almost too sweet, it shocked Rikka to hear her demure sister be so forthright. She had never before heard the ever-tactful Kristine make a whisper of complaint about her marriage or her spouse. Rikka felt suddenly worried, her careless joy drained away. Was there something wrong between these two, both so dear to her?

Before Arnold could respond, Mentz spoke up.

"We met your mother with the little ones on the path as we were coming in. She said to tell you that karsk will be served as soon as we bring you home."

Kristine looked at Rikka's baffled expression and raised her own eyebrows.

"Mother must have been truly enchanted by your program tonight, Rikka. I think this will be the first time she has allowed hard drink served in the house," said Kristine as she pulled Rikka to her feet.

"But she knows well enough that Kris and the other young men keep a bottle in their cupboard," Rikka responded.

Maybe Mama is relaxing her rules for that very reason. Now there will be no excuse for anyone to slip away from the family gathering for a drink at the men's house.

Arnold was keen to steer the conversation away from allusions to his preference for the company of drinking buddies.

"Rikka, I congratulate you," he exclaimed. "You've worked wonders with these children. I know what a chore that can be. It makes me proud that I was their teacher's first music teacher!"

He slipped one arm around Kristine's waist and pulled her close to him and gave Rikka's shoulder a brotherly pat. "I'd like to believe it was my good instruction that turned you into such a wizard. But I see now how much more you learned in Kristiana."

Rikka smiled her thanks. *If Kristine had a dozen husbands, Arnold would still be my favourite brother-in-law.*

She turned to Mentz with elaborate nonchalance.

"I hope it was not too boring for you, sitting through our little concert? You must have heard many wonderful performers in your father's big church in Trondheim."

Mentz's answering smile made Rikka's heart beat a little faster. She looked up at him, her gaze held fast in his.

He sees me. He really sees me.

"It was splendid, just splendid," Mentz said. "I've never heard anything better. Not even in Nidoras Cathedral."

They laughed at his extravagant praise. Mentz protested, "Honestly, I had no idea there was so much talent here."

"Rikka, you deserve all the credit," Kristine said. "How you got the children to learn all those songs … it must have taken hours and hours of practise. Anna Antonsen told me her boys would practise until their fingers bled if you wanted them to. Those kids are in love with you!"

As Rikka laughed in protest, Mentz murmured "I'm sure they are. Who could help but fall in love with her?"

Rikka felt the blood rise in her cheek and turned away, pretending she had not heard him.

They had been tidying up the schoolroom as they talked and now stood back to survey the desks and tables neatly pushed into place, all but one of the lamps extinguished, and the garlands of pine boughs gathered in a fragrant heap to be carried home tomorrow. They would add their fresh colour and fragrance to the great room where the big spruce tree stood waiting to be adorned with candles. Christmas Eve preparations would soon drive all else from their minds. Tomorrow Rikka would help decorate tables, prepare the roasts and platters of cheese, maybe set a secret treat outside to keep any wandering troll from making mischief. Tomorrow the concert would be only a pleasant memory.

An hour ago, Rikka had looked forward to returning home to hot drinks and spicy cookies. But now, she wished time would stop. She wanted to pause and relish this moment, look at it from all angles, cradle it in her hand and marvel at it.

Mentz had taken her arm in his. As they trudged behind Kristine and Arnold through moonlit snow on the silent forested hillside, Rikka felt only regret the walk was not longer, nor the evening colder, so that Mentz might find an excuse to pull her closer and warm her hand in his own.

Chapter 6

Vikna, Norway – 1877

Kristian would rather fish than run the store. Rikka knew that. Everyone in Vikna knew that. Even their mother. And everyone knew that Marie did not accept his decision as final.

Kris might be a strong-willed lad, but, as the women who worked with her were fond of saying, "That Marie now, she has a bone in her nose, alright. When she makes up her mind about something, it will happen."

And they would tell again the stories Rikka grew up hearing, stories of the indomitable Marie grimly struggling to hang on to the business after her husband drowned. With three small children, a farm and a store to manage, many of her neighbours in Vikna had expected her to sell out. Instead she had hung on, saving her son's patrimony for him until he was ready to take over.

"That Kris! He doesn't know his Mama, if he thinks he can change her mind about that," chortled Lotte.

"Some day," Marie said, "Kristian will have had his fill of the ocean."

Until that day, his mother appeared content to see him grow into the life of their village and earn the esteem of workmates and neighbours. Respect came easily enough from this small community of fishermen and farmers, his family's friends, clients and partners for generations. Kristian was readily accepted as a person of consequence in Karstenoya.

All this while still a lad! Rikka fumed. So much deference. So much freedom. So much of all that she desired for herself. Why, when they returned from Kristiania, he was no older than she was now. Yet here she was, still expected to bow her head to her elders and allowed only the dubious privilege of serving as music instructor and church organist.

"Teaching is an honourable profession," Kristine and her mother often reminded her.

Rikka felt her family still treated her like a child, planning her life for her before she had the opportunity to explore other options, limited as they were. In business matters, her mother gave her no more responsibility than one of the workers in the fish house or the dairy women who made their cheeses. As a girl with a married sister and an older brother, she had little status in their household.

She wondered sometimes whether Mentz felt as frustrated in his role as employee. He was expected to perform all the duties assigned him by Marie, who had over the past two years given him more and more responsibility; but the fact remained that he was only a salaried worker, not the owner of the business he managed. It occurred to Rikka that his position was worse than hers. *I at least will always be part of the family. He could be dismissed.*

The thought startled her. What would Vikna be like without Mentz? Although their relationship had quickly slipped back into an indeterminate gray zone of cool correctness, she had to acknowledge that she would prefer he remained one of their circle. No other young man she knew came close to measuring up to him.

Because he never complained, Rikka had to assume he was content with his role as employee. She was as surprised as her mother when Mentz suggested one evening at supper that he might join the ship's crew on their next excursion. One of their regulars, a gray bearded veteran of many voyages, had told Captain Brevig that his old bones could not take another excursion on the North Sea.

"It will likely be the last trip of the season," Mentz said. "And since there is not much work at the store right now, I thought I might be of more use onboard."

As Rikka could have told him, her mother found reasons to object. Marie was always doubtful about any plan not originating with her. But Rikka's eyebrows shot up when even Kris said, albeit with regret, he had already asked an old friend to join them. With Arnold, their other regulars and Captain Brevig, the ship's company was full. Marie then reminded Mentz that they were expecting a ship from down the coast this next week as well. They would surely need him at the store. Only he knew the exact layout of the goods in the warehouse.

"In any case," Marie added, "I will be too busy to take over the store for a few days. I have promised Kristine to help with some sewing for the babies."

That settled it. Kris and Arnold would sail away. Mentz must remain in charge of business on land.

Rikka scowled. She sat straight and tall and looked slowly around the table. It irked her that no one acknowledged that she, Rikka, was perfectly capable of managing the store. In her high clear voice, she said as much to her mother and brother, avoiding looking at Mentz.

"Why shouldn't Mentz go for once? I can do whatever needs to be done at the store."

She waited with chin high for her brother's mocking jibe or her mother's gentle, "Not yet, dear."

To her surprise, after a moment in which Mentz cast a quick frown at her and then turned away while Marie and Kristian exchanged quizzical glances, it seemed they agreed with her.

"You're right," Marie said. "You are quite capable of managing the store for a day or two by yourself, Rikka. It's only that the Alesund men can be a rough bunch. While they mean no harm, they might not be as respectful to a young girl nor trust your knowledge of the goods as much as an older person. Why don't you give Mentz a hand in the store for the next few days? You never know, we might need you to take charge another time."

So it was that Rikka stood on the dock, leaning into the wind as she waved goodbye to Kristian and Arnold and the rest of the crew. She had helped carry the last of their supplies to the ship and wondered about the suspicious clanking of bottles in one of the crates hoisted on board. *But it's not my business to question these men. If I want to be accepted as an adult, I'd best accept the many things that grownups take for granted but do not speak of.*

She wound the woollen shawl around her arms and watched the figures on deck grow smaller as the ship's sails billowed in the bright sunlight. It rounded the cove and was out of sight. She turned and climbed the steep stairway up the sea cliff. Time to begin her new role as Mentz's helper.

Rikka ran up the path to the warehouse. The ship might be out for weeks, or only a few days. Everything depended on the skrei and the weather. A full catch of Arctic cod or a big storm would bring them sailing home. Today the wind blew brisk and steady. She did not think they would see the ship return any time soon.

As the afternoon wore on, Rikka wondered whether Mentz might be indulging in an uncharacteristic sulk. Was he more disappointed than he liked to acknowledge at not being one of the jolly crew just set out to sea? He had barely said a word to her after he handed her a blue-lined notebook and set her to the task of recording inventory.

"It's a job that needs to be done and will give you a sense of the different items of merchandise, too."

After that he became absorbed in his own work, chatting with customers, completing an order. He answered her questions in a business-like way but did nothing to encourage her feeble attempts at conversation.

As the day wore on, she decided he was not despondent, merely indifferent. *He has no feelings. He is content to just do his job. Like an ox.* She, on the other hand, felt bitterly disappointed by his obvious lack of interest in talking to her. When he spoke, which was seldom, he did not joke with her as she heard him do with the young women who seemed to have many reasons to come by the store. He spoke to Rikka in a kindly tone that was even more gentle than his usual courteous manner.

But he's always courteous to women, even ugly old Inga, she thought bitterly. *And I - I am just a foolish girl. He is afraid I will mistake his good manners for something more.*

She blushed to remember her delight that night they had walked home arm in arm from the Christmas concert. She had imagined then that he saw her as a beautiful, talented, and desirable young woman. But ever since, he had treated her with a formality that was almost laughable - *considering that we see each other every day, share the same table - even the same bathtub!*

Is he afraid of being trapped in an early marriage? He need have no fears on that point, she thought. Kristine and Arnold's rapidly expanding family presented her with many good reasons for delaying matrimony. Twins a year old, with their son Arvor only two and Marianne not quite four. Sweet as they were, the amount of time and work accompanying those children was quite enough to give anyone pause. What enormous responsibilities followed marriage!

Besides, Mama seemed determined to keep Rikka, her youngest child, out of the cycle of early marriage and endless childbearing. Rikka suspected her work at the folkeskole was encouraged by Marie for just that reason.

She had not expected to be offered a salaried position as the school's music teacher, and certainly had not expected to enjoy her students as much as she did. She had proven herself a natural teacher. Her pupils acquired enough musical proficiency to delight everyone. Mama, the young scholars, their parents and all the parish residents were happy. Rikka liked her work.

But it was not enough. She did not envision herself as a spinster who filled her life with other people's children. She loved living on the island, she loved teaching her students and sharing her music, but she wanted more. She was only sixteen. She dreamed of romance. Against her will, first her eye and then her heart had settled on Mentz. If he did not want her, she did not want any other man. If he did not want her, she would leave the island. If he did not want her, she would ask her mother to send her back to Kristiana. Maybe her former teachers would offer her work, teaching in the music school. There was talk of a national music school opening. Who knows but she might find opportunity to play for the royal family again? Maybe she could become a concert pianist in the Royal Orchestra!

If Mentz continued to ignore her…

It maddened her to think that everything in her life depended on him, although he seemed hardly to notice her.

A cursory inventory of the warehouse completed, she busied herself sweeping up the main store front room. Her eyes filled with tears as she thought how sad it would be to leave this island, just because of a young man's blind, stubborn, oxlike indifference. Mentz opened the door at the same moment she reached for the door handle, intending to brush the pile of dust and shavings outside. She laughed as he bowed solemnly as though making way for royalty while she sent the dirt flying over the stone steps.

"Thank you, kind sir!"

A friendly joking relationship would be easier to bear than his avoiding her. Maybe if he could chat with her as easily as he did with other girls, he would like her better.

"You don't need to do that, you know," he said as she hung the broom on its hook behind the door. "Inga comes in every afternoon and cleans up after us."

"Well, she doesn't do much of a job, does she." Rikka felt spiteful. As if she would take homely old Inga's place!

"Maybe not. Her eyes are not the best and getting no better with years. But she is proud of being independent and working to earn your mother's gift of bed and board. You don't want to take that away from her, do you."

It was a statement of fact and needed no reply. Rikka felt ashamed. It occurred to her that she had never thought of old Inga as anything other than a slightly annoying piece of furniture, something you were obliged to put up with but not deserving your attention. The old woman had been part of her mother's household at Vikna for as long as Rikka could recall, knitting in her low rocker by the fireplace. She had gradually dropped from her position as kitchen helper to boarder, doing only the lightest tasks. Her arthritic back bent her body almost double. And, Rikka realized, old Inga only went to the store in the late afternoon after she had spent several hours toasting her back in her chimney corner "to get the kinks out" as she said. Mentz had seen all this and was as kind and gentle in his manner with the old woman as if she were his own grandmother. It occurred to her that despite the large place he occupied in her consciousness, she really knew very little about what went on in Mentz's mind.

"You are a good person, Mentz!"

It burst from her lips without intention, as spontaneous and uncluttered a remark as she had ever uttered to him. It was a novel experience to think of him in some other context than his alarming affect on her pulse rate and imagination.

"Thank you, my lady. I try to do my duty." Mentz grinned at her. "Just as you do yours, helping your sister and your mother. And of course, all that you do at the school with the children. I don't think I have ever told you how very much I admire your talent and how you use it to give everyone so much pleasure."

Rikka was accustomed to expressions of appreciation from the parents of her students, and usually brushed them off with a deprecating remark, bearing in mind her mother's warning about 'pride of self'. This was the first time - no, the second time! - that Mentz had taken any notice of her accomplishments. She felt a little embarrassed and wondered whether he thought her own spontaneous expression of appreciation deserved a response in kind. As though reading her thoughts, he went on.

"I admit, I'm no judge of music in general. But I would never tire of hearing you play."

Rikka felt she needed to resume the playful bantering tone.

"Why, thank you again! You are not often so nice to me!"

He frowned, as though her joking remark had hurt him.

"I am sorry if I've ever seemed unkind to you. Sometimes it is necessary to say and do much less than a man might like to."

Rikka stood motionless, gazing up at him, willing him with all her heart to see in her eyes everything she wanted to hear him say.

Instead, he took her hand and said, "It would be enough for now to know you are my friend."

She smiled, her heart and her eyes aglow. *Yes, that will have to be enough for now.*

Chapter 7

Vikna, 1883

The afternoon faded. Raindrops splattered her shoulders, showering from the overhanging branches of the ash tree that sheltered the bench where she sat. Dampness soaked through the thick dark wool of her shawl. She shivered.

Rikka stood up and walked slowly through the cemetery, head down, into the strengthening wind, hands tucked into the long sleeves of her white blouse. This time of year, wet cold weather made her heart ache with sadness. Her body seemed determined to remind her of all that her mind tried to forget. So much had changed and yet the pain had not lessened. When she could no longer bear it, she made her excuses to Mentz, left the warehouse, and hurried off to the cemetery to sit by the only tangible reminder of her brother. They had placed his headstone beside her father's. Arnt Kristofersen Lund, 1821-1862. Kristian Arntsen Lund, 1853 - 1877. Father and son, both taken too young, both taken by the terrible power of the sea.

As a child, she had mourned for a father she had never known. *Kristine and Kris remembered him, but I grew up thinking his death was somehow connected to my birth - and those stories old Nils used to tell me about changelings and trolls.*

Her grief for Kris was both more real and more agonizing. She had known her brother, had fought and played and laughed with him. His life was part of hers.

What was worse, she believed she might have prevented his death.

Six years to the day since the accident. A calamity that need never have happened. *It is my fault, I should have confronted them, those men, Arnold and Captain Brevig and Kris, especially Kris. I should have shamed them into leaving the liquor behind. I guessed what Kris had slipped into that crate, what was making that clanking sound as he set it down on the deck. He might be alive today if I'd spoken up.*

Would they have listened to me? I wanted so badly to be treated as one of the grownups. I was afraid they would just laugh at my qualms, not care that I knew. Kristine or Mother would have stopped them. But I was only 16. Just a girl. A cowardly fearful foolish girl!

In what seemed to her now an unbelievably distant time, in the few enchanted days before they knew of the shipwreck, she and Mentz had come to their secret understanding. She had imagined a deliciously long engagement, hours of stolen kisses and confidential walks hand in hand along the seashore. There would be family celebrations and community festivals and music, lots of music, and she would be the centre, the admired, the darling of the household. She would be Mentz's beloved.

Instead, their world had collapsed almost before she had dreamed it.

Within a week of that transformative afternoon in the warehouse, only days after the storm which had not seemed so very bad to those at home in Vikna, word came with the crew of a returning ship. None of them, not she nor her mother nor Kristine, could comprehend news of the tragedy until at last they stood side by side sobbing as the shroud-wrapped bodies were carried ashore. Five men, all taken in their prime. One her sister's husband. One her only brother. Captain Brevig and two more crew members. All five mourned by every home in the community.

Then the whispers began.

"That young Kris, you know how he liked his liquor. Took as much as he wanted from his mother's store. No, of course she didn't know. Or pretended not to."

"Yes, Brevig was captain. He knew better. Kept brandy for emergencies, as usual, but ran a dry ship. But how could he gainsay the owner's son?"

"Oh, their hands, you should have seen their poor hands! Torn to shreds by the rocks they were, cut clear to the bone as they tried to pull themselves out of the waves. Their faces battered beyond recognition."

"They were all blind drunk. If it hadn't been for that demon drink, they might have seen the weather coming, sailed into harbour like others did."

"They would all be alive today, if they had not been drunk."

"It was Kris Lund."

Not surprising that soon after, the Parish passed an ordinance forbidding the sale of spirits in Vikna. And if it hurt the Lund family more than most, their store being the only supplier of liquor, not surprising that no one raised an objection. Least of all Marie Lund who became greyer and thinner almost overnight and seemed determined to make the rest of her life a penance for the lives lost.

Kristine in catatonic grief, Marie alternately praying and weeping, Rikka alone saw that Kristine and Arnold's children were the innocent sufferers. She made them her charges. Marianne at four and Arvor, only three, were keenly aware of the pain surrounding them and wandered like confused little ghosts about their formerly happy home. The year-old twins, cared for by their nanny, were less affected. At least, that was what Rikka believed.

Then little Ragna came down with a fever.

A more experienced nursemaid would have known it was serious. In normal times, Marie and Kristine would have wrapped the child in cooling cloths to bring down the fever, would have used what folk medicine they had, would have watched her day and night. By the time the frightened girl carried the limp child to her mother, it was too late. Baby Ragna died in Kristine's arms that evening.

Terrible as it was, that was the catalyst that jolted Kristine out of her stupor and brought the family together again. She gathered her other children to her and wept with them, then dried her eyes, straightened her back and took charge of her home.

Marie, too, stirred from her lethargy of grief to discover that Mentz had laboured night and day to save her business for her. He salvaged what trade he could from their tottering commerce, which had fallen off drastically, despite lingering sympathy for the family, when customers learned their source of schnapps had dried up. Rikka had tried to share the load and had loved him more each day as she saw all he did for her family. It was balm to her aching heart to hear her mother say to Mentz, "How could we have managed without you?" and to feel her mother's reassuring hand on her shoulder.

Rikka prayed that those years be kept in the past, never to return. She would always carry regrets, and secretly blame herself, but it seemed to her that God and the universe had exacted enough pain. Maybe she had finally served her full sentence. Might she not be forgiven and allowed to live in peace and happiness? Sometimes it almost seemed as though that were the case.

Gradually, a sense of peace and purpose returned to each of them. It soothed Rikka's heart to see Kristine with her children, her red-blond head bent to listen to the childish prattle of little Harald, teaching Arvor his letters or vainly endeavouring to interest Marianne in the fine art of needlework. No one enjoyed the sight more than Odin.

Odin came into their lives almost without Rikka noticing, so wrapped up was she in the needs of her family. He was tall and well-built, possessor of a fine baritone singing voice, a gentle manner and an almost childlike spirituality. He entered the community as schoolteacher and church singer. Before long he knew everyone from youngsters to oldsters by name. He saw Kristine mourning her husband, and he saw her come back to life for the sake of her children. Rikka played for the church services, and he led the singing. It was only natural that Marie should invite him to join their family table for Sunday dinner. It was only natural that he should take to little Arvor and that little Arvor should take to him. It was only natural that he and Kristine should walk together in the summer evenings while the children played around them. And when they serenely announced they would be married in the fall, it seemed the most natural thing in the world.

Marianne had attached herself firmly to Mentz in the months after her father's drowning and merely tolerated the growing presence of this other man. When she understood that her mother and Odin would soon be husband and wife, she had a wonderful idea. Seizing hold of Mentz's hand she announced, "If Mama is marrying Odin, because she loves him best, I will marry Mentz. Because I love him best."

Everyone laughed. Mentz hugged her and thanked her for the great compliment.

"But you know, Marianne, you are only six years old and look at me. I am twenty-one. By the time you are a grownup, I will be an old man and you won't want me."

Marianne protested that she could wait to grow up and then marry him. When she caught his eyes turn to Rikka, she ran from the room and no one saw her again until evening, when she returned solemn and red-eyed.

Rikka remembered this and smiled as she hurried back towards the store and Mentz. Marianne was 12 years old now and as aware as everyone else in the community that Rikka and Mentz had an understanding. No one doubted they would marry … if not now, some day. For Rikka, that day could not come soon enough. She hungered to claim his attention, have him all to herself, to look after his every need, day and night. But Mentz patiently explained to her that he first must prove himself someone more than her mother's employee.

"I don't want anyone to think I am taking advantage of a tragedy to marry for wealth," he said. "Or stepping into your brother's shoes. When I have built up a nest egg, I will buy a share in your family business as your mother has offered."

Rikka protested that he had already proven his worth, her mother knew how much their family owed to Mentz's careful management. Almost as soon as Marie had understood how things were between him and Rikka, she had offered him a partnership.

"No one could ever think badly of you," Rikka insisted. "Only look at how people come to you when they need help with anything. You built Jon's sloop while he sat watching. You finished Gerta's roof for her after Ulf got sick. Everyone trusts you and likes you."

She flung her arms around his neck. "But no one else loves you as much as I do."

They were alone in the store, it was the end of the day, and for a few minutes Mentz forgot his self-imposed rule of treating Rikka as though her mother were always in the room with them, watching.

Then he held her at arm's length and spoke in a solemn tone, "Even you don't know everything about me."

"What don't I know?" challenged Rikka.

"I am not the kind, generous man you imagine I am. I have been hiding something from you for months and it is time I confess."

He spoke so seriously that for a moment Rikka feared he had some dreadful secret to reveal.

"I never charge when a friend or neighbour asks for help, that is true. But ..."

A huge grin drove away all severity from his face.

"But neither do I deny them the pleasure of rewarding me as they see fit. Sometimes with a plate of cookies.

Sometimes with krone. Real money! We need wait no longer. I will speak to your mother tonight."

His last words were muffled as she flung herself into his arms and pressed her lips to his.

Marianne is right – he is worth waiting for.

Chapter 8

Vikna, 1890

"Mentz! Uncle Mentz!"

As usual, Marianne could be heard before she was seen. She was not a girl to go through life unnoticed.

Rikka glanced up from the laundry tub and made a most unladylike snort of annoyance. *That girl is always underfoot, filling the room with her foolish exuberance. She runs from one thing to another as though she thinks the world is here for her entertainment. No wonder the children adore her. She exhausts my patience. She simply cannot be depended upon!*

An image floated before Rikka's eyes of the raw wool still up in the loft, piled in the basket by the spinning wheel. Last week Kristine had sent Marianne to help Rikka with the spinning. It was not many hours before Marianne found some excuse to run off on a more important errand. She had left the job half-done. Rikka had a sinking feeling that she would have to either pull one of the dairy women from her work, which would leave them short-handed for the cheese-making, or finish all the spinning herself. *Not that I'd mind that, if I had time. There is too much work and not enough hands.* Half a dozen more families had left the island for America just this year. And naturally it was not the elderly or infirm who chose to emigrate, but the youngest and strongest workers. They were sorely missed.

Marianne might be such a help to them all, now that she was almost grown up, if only she were more dependable and less flighty.

If only she were more like Kristine. Or me.

Rikka's own work never ended. After seven years of marriage, she and Mentz had four children and her thickened body announced to all and sundry that another was on the way. The duties attendant upon running their sprawling household consumed her life. It seemed to her sometimes that her own hopes and dreams had always been swallowed up by the needs of her family. Had there ever been a time when she did not have a child hanging from her skirt?

Lotte straightened up from spreading the linens to dry on the low wooden fence surrounding the back garden. Her eyes followed Rikka's gaze. "Marianne is getting to be a fine-looking woman," she remarked.

"Seems like yesterday she was just a little bit of a thing, her eyes so big and hungry, always following you or Mentz around the store. That was after the accident of course … she was missing her papa so bad …"

Her voice trailed away as she noticed Rikka's expression.

"Yes of course Marianne is attached to us. All my sister's children are as dear to us as our own."

She did love her sister's children. Marianne had been such a funny bright-eyed little girl. Now – well, now this coltish young woman had become an annoyance, a stone in her shoe, a reminder of her own lost carefree youth.

"I remember when that child was born," Lotte continued. "We girls were so worried about Kristine – the first baby is the hardest, they say."

Childbirth and marriage were Lotte's two favourite topics. Having neither husband nor child, she regarded Rikka's family as her own.

"Now that baby is all grown up and has ten brothers and sisters."

"Only two full brothers," Rikka corrected her. "Kristine and Odin's children are her half-brothers and sisters."

"You and your sister are blessed for sure," said Lotte. "'All those babies! It's true what they say – 'when troubles come, it's your family that supports you.' You and Kristine will never be left alone."

"Likely not," Rikka replied, thinking sourly *I would not mind being left alone. Sometimes.*

Then, recalling that poor Lotte would need always to rely on the goodwill of others for a home, she felt ashamed. *Family is a blessing. I should just feel grateful!*

She had healthy children. Their business was prospering once again. What did she have to complain of? Her household, like her mother's before her, consisted of more than twenty souls, not only her immediate family but many of the people employed by them, dairy women and livestock men, cook and scullery maid and often a girl hired to help with the children. Lotte did most of the drudge work, including the laundry. But Rikka was particular about the baby things. The fine hardanger embroidery her mother had worked on her namesake Marie's little smocks could not be entrusted to Lotte.

The last dress hung to dry sparkling white in the sunshine, she dried her hands on her apron and followed Marianne down the stairs.

Marianne had taken the last few steps in a leap, skirts flying, and landed almost in Mentz's arms as he came out of the store. Laughing, he caught her up and whirled her around, then set her down with a kiss on her tanned cheek.

"What is your hurry this morning, Miss Marianne?"

"Oh, Uncle Mentz, can't you guess? What have I been waiting for these past weeks? I finally got my letter from America - and the answer is "Yes!'"

"Jon has agreed. You may stay with them?"

"Yes, yes, just as you told me he would. Thank you so much for writing to him, he and his wife have agreed to all of it, they have invited me to stay with them until I can find work and a place of my own. Their letter sounds so friendly. I think he must be just like you!"

"Oh, much smarter than I am, I think. Smart enough to go to America while he was still a boy and make his own way. When I last saw him, we were both lads. Now I suppose you will leave us forever, too. And we will tell stories of our Marianne, the wild child who never walked when she could run, never talked if she could sing. We will grow old on opposite sides of this ocean."

"Uncle Mentz, how can you be so gloomy? You know I will come back here to see you." Marianne turned at the sound of Rikka's footsteps on the stairs. "And Mama and my dear Aunt Rikka. And Marmar and all the little ones!"

She continued in a calmer tone. "Anyway, Mama will not let me go until I am sixteen. She thinks I am still a child."

Mentz glanced over Marianne's curly auburn crown and directed a wry grin at Rikka. "How unfair of her. Anyone can plainly see that you are a most properly brought up young lady."

Marianne punched his arm. "You know Mama and Odin are still talking of emigrating. But Mama wants to wait a while, until the children are older and can help with farm work. America is the land of opportunity! Odin says Harold and Arvor will be able to get homesteads of their own!"

"And I suppose you, too, will have your own farm?" Rikka's tone dripped sarcasm. Marianne seemed not to notice.

"Oh no, not me! I will go to Chicago. I am going to learn English and study medicine. Someday I will be a doctor in a big hospital there. I intend to be a modern woman - not live with a baby always in my arms!"

"No, I don't suppose you would like that. Not a fine lady like you!"

Rikka had not meant to sound so harsh. She had intended merely to remind Mentz by her sedate presence that while Marianne was his niece, it would be well for him to keep in mind that she was also a lively young lady. As Rikka often pointed out to him, people liked to gossip. Marianne was altogether too attractive to be hanging about him the way Rikka had seen her do. But Marianne's implied disparagement of her role as wife and mother made her blood hot. Was not she, Rikka, the one of whom great things had been expected? Had she not had her own dreams of a career when she was Marianne's age, dreams grander than anything Marianne conceived of with her pathetic little plan of getting to America and somehow becoming a doctor? What could the silly girl do, alone in a strange land? No doubt she too would end up with a child in each arm just like her mother, and her mother before her!

Mentz stared at Rikka, startled by her rudeness. Rikka glared back, daring him to reprimand her in front of this impudent girl. Marianne, unaware that she had caused offense, continued bubbling over with her exciting news.

"Aunt Rikka, you must come to the Pink House and see the letter. Imagine, all the way from America! And soon I will go there too!"

Mentz spoke as though conscious of a need to assert his own place as head of his household and ultimate authority over his wife.

"Yes, Rikka, why not go with her now. Lotte can watch the children. If you think little Marie may need to nurse, well, let

Marianne carry her for you. Don't weary yourself needlessly."

"Mama and Marmar haven't seen you all week, Aunt Rikka, and I know they would love to have coffee with you. Do come!"

Near tears with suppressed annoyance and weariness, Rikka knew that refusing would seem childish in Mentz' eyes.

"Yes, alright," she agreed, meeting his steady gaze with vacant eyes. Turning to Marianne, her tone curt, she said, "Come with me and get the baby ready while I tell Lotte and the others what needs to be done this morning. We will take the other children with us to play with their cousins."

As Marianne strode along the path, baby Marie astride one hip and five-year-old Ingeborg hurrying to keep pace with her adored cousin, she never stopped talking and laughing. She did not seem to notice Rikka's silence.

Rikka scarcely heard the girl, so deep was she in her own angry thoughts. Everything about pretty, exuberant Marianne grated on her feelings. *That girl! She never has had one moment of care for my feelings. To her I am just the old auntie who oversees the preparation of feasts for Christmas or Easter, plays the church organ every Sunday worship service. The one who makes music for every special occasion but always with a frown on her face and a child on her knee.*

It was not supposed to turn out this way.

Rikka self-consciously smoothed her hand over her brow. She knew her hair was as thick and lustrous as ever, her figure still strong and erect. Her hands were roughened but her fingers, still supple, had gained greater skill than in that long ago time when she had played for the Queen. *Why should I resent this silly girl chattering beside me?*

Why indeed. It was not the fault of Marianne, the little girl whose dreadful need had stolen a tenderness that Rikka had expected to be all her own. For only a few days it had seemed that her youthful dreams were about to be fulfilled. She had basked in Mentz's love, wrapped in a cocoon of happiness, her temper perfect, her beauty supreme. Then death and disaster came in the night and her world changed. Her own wishes no longer mattered to anyone, not even herself. It was as though she had wakened from a dream and been jolted back to reality after indulging in a childish play-acting. She and Mentz submerged their own needs, even their own sorrow, to help carry the burden of the weaker ones, her stricken mother and her sister's small children. And this child Marianne had especially clung to Mentz, as though he were the rock of her salvation.

I did not resent that, Rikka told herself fiercely. *I did all that was needed and more, gave of myself for my family's survival. But now everyone, even Mentz, expects that of me and no one ever asks me how I feel, what I think or want. Do I even know myself? Maybe I have become only what I do. A drudge incapable of being or thinking anything.*

She resolutely shook aside these thoughts as they entered the flower-bordered house yard of Kristine and Odin's home. The Pink House, as they called it, had one kind of flower or another blooming by its big front door from springtime through autumn. Roses cascaded from a trellis and filled the air with fragrance. Kristine greeted them at the door. She took baby Marie from Marianne and said, "Take Ingeborg and the little boys to see the kittens. The other children are playing back there somewhere. Keep them busy so Mama and Rikka and I can have our coffee in peace, will you, dear?"

Gratefully Rikka sank into a chair opposite her mother, who had claimed her namesake as her rightful charge and now cuddled the baby on her lap. Rikka smiled at the sight of her mother's wrinkled cheeks creased with laughter as she bent over the baby's dimpled face and silky curls.

"She has your smile and your eyes, Mama."

"Of course, she does! One Marie at the end of her life, one at the beginning. We Maries must stick together."

Suddenly serious, her mother turned to her. "Rikka, you know Kristine and Odin are planning to take their family to America. You and Mentz are not talking of any such thing, are you?"

"No, Mother, how could we think of leaving you? No, Kristine and Odin may feel they need more opportunities for themselves and their children, but for us, why, the store is doing so well! Business is growing all the time. Has Mentz discussed with you his plan to build another store? To carry weekly supplies for the islands north? He has bought the rights to two small islands a day's journey up the coast, just big rocks really, but between them they make a fair harbour so ships can get supplies there instead of coming all the way back here."

Rikka felt a sudden rush of pleasure that she had news to share that was at least as exciting and certainly more important than her niece's letter from America. Kristine and her mother exclaimed at the news. Her own pride restored, Rikka sipped her coffee and made the requisite sounds of interest, commiseration, and delight as Kristine expounded on the prospects for her family across the sea with almost as much enthusiasm as Marianne had displayed.

Rikka glanced out the window and saw Marianne laughing as she rinsed off the little boys under the pump in the side yard. Apparently Aksel and Asbjorne, along with their cousins, found the weanlings in the pigpen more interesting than the kittens. *Oh well, it's nearly noon … time to return home.* Her mother also rose and donned her bonnet and cloak.

"Kristine don't expect me back until sunset. I will walk to the store with Rikka and have a little chat with Mentz. If he is planning on expanding our business, I want to have a hand in it too."

So it was that within the month, Mentz had begun construction of a cod-oil processing plant on the island of Helligholmen. Before another year passed, he had, with his mother-in-law as silent partner, bought a small steamship. No longer dependent on the vagaries of weather, his ship ferried supplies and passengers up and down the coastal villages within a hundred kilometers of Vikna.

His neighbours were not surprised. He was an enterprising man, always trying his hand at something new. He had been the first on the islands to try out a system of irrigation that had increased the yield of hayfields so that their farm's dairy production had doubled. Others now followed his lead. It was only natural that he should find innovations to expand his shipping business as well. If his windmills had not shocked his neighbours, neither would his steamship. And they reminded each other over a sip of strong coffee sometimes strengthened with a secret nip of home brew, he did, after all, have the backing of his wife's mother. Nor were they surprised at the name of the steamship, named not for his wife, but for his mother-in-law, widow Marie Lund. The *Marie* steamed proudly into Vikna that autumn.

The following year, as the ship steamed away from Vikna for a trip south to Bergen for supplies, a proud and excited young lady marched on board with her steamer trunk. In Marianne's valise was a ticket for passage to New York, money for the journey, and the address of Mentz's brother in Chicago.

The exodus had begun.

Chapter 9

Vikna, 1895 -1896

"Ingeborg! Come, take the baby!"

Rikka handed baby Ruth to ten-year-old Ingeborg, then hurriedly buttoned her gown and pulled her apron back into place. These hours spent nursing her babies had once been her favourite times of the day, when she gave herself up to the simple animal pleasure of holding a warm sweet baby suckling at her breast. Now it seemed just one more burden added to the incessant busyness of her days.

Six times she had given birth. Six babies to be cared for, fretted over, nursed and weaned. Each one loved. Each one growing and revealing unique traits. Each one needing something different from her. Fiercely proud as she was of her strong handsome brood, sometimes she felt overwhelmed.

Today was just such a day. She forced herself to straighten her aching back and gave an impatient shrug of her shoulders.

Her gaze lingered for a moment on Ingeborg, bent lovingly over baby Ruth. Her blond hair was just beginning to darken to chestnut, her complexion still the pink and white of childhood. *Fresh and tender as a summer rose. She will no doubt be a better mother than I am; it seems in her nature. More like Kristine than me. Is it because they are both the eldest? Ingeborg always has a baby brother or sister to play with and make much of, as Kristine did … whereas when I was her age, I hardly noticed babies. Never cared much for them, either, never cooed over newborns as some girls did.*

In the weeks after Ruth's birth, Rikka had at first been amazed and grateful for her daughter's eagerness to help care for the baby, then grew to depend on it. Now, she realized, she simply took Ingeborg's help for granted.

But what else am I to do? She certainly was not the first mother to turn her daughter into nursemaid for the younger children. How else could a woman who gave birth almost yearly take care of the many duties needed to keep a large household fed and clothed? Spinning and weaving, knitting and sewing. Salting pork and drying fish. Making gjetost or other cheeses from creamy goat's milk. Endlessly supervising the work of others.

Never time to run down the path and talk with Mentz. Never time for a conversation. Never a minute alone with him, except in bed.

And in bed, Mentz was never one to waste time talking. Even after a dozen years of marriage.

Rikka gave her head a shake and stepped outside. The steamship *Marie* rested dockside in the tranquil blue of the bay. She could see two men on board giving the deck a final scrub and polish. It looked as though someone had hung banners or flags along the railing. Farewells here, then more farewells in Trondheim. She had dreaded this day for months. She did not expect to see her sister ever again. Kristine's family were, finally, leaving for America.

There would be few of her dear old friends left in Karstenoya after today. A steady stream of islanders had left as the North Sea fishery dwindled, the herring as well as the usually reliable winter harvest of cod. Frequent letters arrived in the island from the expatriates, firing others with dreams of opportunities offered in the lumber camps and farms of North America. It was nearly two years since Kristine's husband Odin had left, going alone, declaring he could not take his family into the wilds of the new world without first ensuring he could make a home for them there. Now he had written that the time was right. Kristine and their children would leave today to join him. Her boys from her first marriage would be able to file on their own homesteads in Minnesota ... *But why do I think of them as boys? Arvor and Harald are young men! I must be getting old myself to still think of my grown-up nephews as "boys". They are the age Mentz was when he first came to work for Mama. Older than Marianne when she went all alone to Chicago.*

Marianne had returned after her four years in America a little thinner and much quieter. She had kept in touch with family and friends at Vikna faithfully until the last year, when, after an exuberant letter announcing her engagement to a young intern at the hospital where she trained as a nurse, communication had inexplicably stopped. The next time she wrote, it was to tell them that her husband had died, and she was coming home a widow. It was not until she got off the steamer in Trondheim they discovered she had not come home alone. Rikka knew there had been some counting on fingers and raised eyebrows among the women of the island, but after all, these things happen, and sympathy for Marianne was high. Not many weeks had passed before Marianne was bouncing around the islands like a high-spirited child again, leaving her mother Kristine or one of the other women in their household to watch the baby. Even with a child, she did not lack for suitors. Before her son's first birthday, Marianne was married to a young fisherman from Rorvik. Rorvik, the largest town on the islands and located on the innermost island of Vikna, was separated from their island, outer Vikna, by an ocean channel. By no stretch of the imagination could it be considered at their doorstep; and yet it brought Marianne close enough to Karstenoya that the force of her energy disrupted Rikka's serenity.

Last week Marianne had arrived for one more visit with her mother and siblings before they departed for the new world. Impulsive as always, she had declared her intention to accompany them as far as Trondheim.

"Marmar, you must come too," she said to Marie. Her grandmother was delighted with the plan and Marianne promised Kristine she would then see her grandmother safely back home to Vikna.

"But what about little Karl, Marianne?" Marie asked. "You will not take him along, will you? Babies can be such an inconvenience at times like this."

All eyes turned to Rikka. She was kept close at home with her own little ones, her belly bulging with the telltale signs of another new life. The choice was clear. All agreed that Marianne's baby should be left in Rikka's capable care. It was, after all, only for a few days. After seeing Kristine's family embark from Trondheim, Marianne and Marie would return to Vikna with Mentz in the *Marie*.

Now Rikka forced herself to smile and greet other well-wishers as they hurried down the path past her door, eager to make the departure a festive send-off. Everyone seemed in a holiday mood. Her mother had already gone on board and Rikka suspected that her namesake, little Marie, had tagged along, hoping to stow away in the confusion. Ingeborg followed her mother outside, baby Ruth cradled against her shoulder while she rhythmically patted the baby's back. Rikka felt a pang of sympathy for her eldest child.

"Ingeborg, I know you wanted to go along to see them off at Trondheim. But I need your help with the babies while everyone is away. Karl's milk teeth are giving him trouble. You know how fussy babies are while they're teething!"

Tears spilled down Ingeborg's cheeks. "But Mama, Gudrun and Signe are my best friends in all the world, and they are going so far away, almost the other side of the world. I will never ever see them again. And Auntie Kristine! Why should Aksel and Asbjorne get to go along with Papa? Just because they are boys!"

Ingeborg's voice choked in a sob, but she managed to add, "Marianne said I could come with them!"

Rikka's heart, softened by her child's tears, hardened a little at Marianne's name. *Ingeborg always craves time with Marianne. God forbid she grow up to be like her!*

But Marmar Marie would watch over Ingeborg and make sure she came to no harm. It was, after all, only for a few days. *A day to sail to Trondheim, a day there, then a day home. Why should not our eldest child be given this treat, as well as her brothers? Why should she have to miss out just because she is a girl?*

That thought decided Rikka.

"Oh, put the baby in her cradle and run get your good dress. You can change onboard. I will let Marmar and Marianne know you are coming with them."

Ingeborg squealed a delighted, "Tuk, Mama" and turned back to the house. Rikka called after her, "Tell Lotte she needs to look sharp today and watch both the babies for me."

After the bustle and noise and confusion of getting everyone safely on board, Rikka and Kristine sharing a last tearful hug, Rikka gently extracted a protesting Marie from Marmar's arms and carried her ashore. The gangplank was raised. Rikka stood on the dock waving as the racket of the steam engine revved into half-throttle. She could see Mentz fine and handsome in his black coat smiling at her from the helm, their two little boys standing straight and proud beside him. Ingeborg stood between her cousins Signe and Gudrun, their arms entwined. Marianne, Kristine and her mother stood behind them, perfect representations of three stages of womanhood – young mother, mature wife, elderly widow.

Most likely the last time our family will stand together.

She watched until the ship steamed out of the harbour. Silence descended on the island, the sea, the sky. A breeze moved gently over the waters, as though the world breathed a sigh. Rikka did too.

Then Lotte called to her that Marianne's baby had awoken, and she could not stop his crying. Rikka returned to the house and her many duties.

The afternoon passed, and so busy did she keep herself with necessary daily tasks that she hardly gave a thought to the travellers. It would be late tomorrow before they reached Trondheim, and another day before Mentz would start the journey back home. It was quiet. She missed the usual bustle of activity around the yard and children running in and out of the house. Little Hjordis and Marie played quietly with their dolls, mimicking their mother in her care of the two babies. With everyone busy on the farm or at the store, for once they were quite alone, except for Lotte.

Poor Lotte! Never had she been able to keep her mind on any but the simplest of tasks, and now with the years piling on her shoulders, she moved so slowly that Rikka sometimes complained to Mentz she was more of a boarder than a helper. Rikka well knew that she would be hard put to keep her from her rocking chair in the chimney corner long enough to help with anything. The most Rikka could hope for was that she would watch the little girls at play and hold a fussy baby.

In spite of her resolve to remain calm and cheerful, Rikka felt a niggling worm of resentment eating into her mind. She had not wanted to go on this farewell journey to Trondheim, she told herself. She was glad for the opportunity to do this last service for Kristine, giving her a few more days with her mother and daughter. But might they not at least have shown some appreciation? It seemed everyone … sister, mother, niece, even her own husband … had taken her staying behind for granted. Maybe they were even relieved that she would stay away. Maybe they had whispered among themselves, "It is best if Rikka not come." Maybe they had observed her cool manner and dismissive attitude towards Marianne. Maybe Mentz had suggested Rikka might care for Marianne's baby, in compensation for her coldness.

What is so admirable about a girl who marries far from home ... if she indeed married! ... and then expects her family to help pick up the pieces of her shattered life?

She pedaled the cream churn with more vigour than usual.

By evening, Rikka was tired but satisfied that everything that absolutely had to have attention had been attended to. The butter had been churned and one of the young dairymaids had patted it into molds and stored it in the icehouse. The eggs had been picked, the chickens fed, the goats milked and turned out to graze again. Mentz had told the other workers to take tomorrow as a holiday and the day after that was Sunday, so only household chores would need attention. Rikka decided she could leave Lotte to watch Marianne's little Karl playing on the rug and baby Ruth, fed and content, asleep in her cradle. Hjordis and Marie she had tucked into bed right after their supper of milk porridge. Rikka suddenly yearned for few moments to walk in the cool evening air, freshen her face with a splash of cold water, and enjoy the quiet and stillness.

Karl tripped over the wooden toy horse he had been playing with and fell heavily. Still a toddler, tumbles like this were frequent and no cause for concern. He whimpered, and as Rikka bent to pick him up, he began to wail - not the loud indignant wail of a sturdy boy-child, but the thin and raspy sobs of a sick baby. She felt the heat radiating from his little body, saw the mucous running from his nose. Had he been feverish earlier today and she too busy to notice? *But children get sick so suddenly. Well and happy one minute, burning with fever the next. It must be some little ailment that will pass as quickly as it has come on.*

Her vivid memory of baby Ragna's illness and death still haunted her. *But that was long ago when I was young and lacked experience. Since then, I have nursed my babies through croupe and whooping cough, fevers and rashes. Marianne's little Karl is safer with me than with any other mother in all the islands.*

All that night, the child fretted and fussed. His breathing became raspier, and it seemed he felt some respite from his discomfort only when Rikka cradled him in her arms and walked the floor with him. She summoned Lotte from her bed to build up the fire, bring the kettle to a boil and sprinkle in pungent herbs, thyme and bergamot, so the steam would carry the medicine to his struggling lungs. She picked up Ruth from her cradle when she began fussing, then realized that she had done so without washing her hands or changing her apron, precautions against infection that she conscientiously followed ever since reading a pamphlet by a doctor in Bergen. *Now little Ruth will be sick too.* She was exhausted and on the verge of tears.

Morning came with no respite from the fever. The day passed in a blur. Chickens complained in their coop, the store remained locked and shuttered, the little girls given into Lotte's charge to play in the house yard for the morning but then brought indoors where she could keep half an eye on them herself. She was used to being pulled in a dozen directions at once by her own children, but now, most of her attention was on Marianne's child. Nothing else mattered when there was a sick baby. The baby grew more and more lethargic, his temperature mounting as the afternoon passed, his breathing growing more laboured with each passing hour. Rikka wracked her brain for other remedies she might try and wished that she had not relied so much on her mother to supply a folk remedy for every ill.

I should have paid attention and asked more questions. What would Mother do? She watched baby Ruth closely, dreading some sign that the child had picked up the infection. Lotte remained glued to her rocking chair, sometimes holding one and sometimes the other baby but not daring to contradict Rikka's strict command that she not move from her chair while holding a baby for fear she might drop the child.

It was dusk on the third day when the steamship whistle sounded at the entrance to the harbour. Mentz was back, and with him, her mother and Marianne. First checking on Ruth in her cradle, she handed Karl to Lotte.

"Don't move from your chair, Lotte. Just hold Karl, like so. With his head up and the blankets snug around him. I will be back in a few minutes."

She dashed out the door and down the path to the stairs.

Mentz saw her coming, saw anxiety in every line of her body, and, handing the rope he was fastening to the wharf post to one of his crew, hurried to meet her at the bottom of the stairs.

"Marianne's baby," she gasped. "He's so sick and I do not know what more I can do."

Marianne and her mother followed him, with Ingeborg, Aksel and Asbjorne close behind.

"Oh, hurry, please hurry," Rikka sobbed.

Minutes later, the women and Mentz entered the house to a scene almost exactly as Rikka had left it. Rikka's baby Ruth peacefully napping in her cradle. Marie and Hjordis playing with their dolls.

Lotte sitting in her rocker, holding Marianne's baby, the firelight flickering shadows over her bent frame and wrinkled face, now stained with tears.

"I did just as you said, Rikka, and did not move except to rock the baby a little. And I thought he had fallen asleep, poor little thing."

Then Rikka realized what was missing from the scene.

The rasping wheeze of the baby's breath.

* * *

Her world was gray, inside and out.

Had there ever been a time she was happy? Mired in despondency, Rikka doubted the possibility of happiness in this world or the next. A cold nagging voice repeated over and over, it is your fault. You are to blame.

Baby Karl was dead. Marianne would scarcely look at her. Kristine was gone, far away to America. Letters informing her of the tragedy followed her across the ocean but would take weeks to reach her. Rikka lay awake at night torturing herself with imagined scenes of Kristine's reaction when she heard the news. *Kristine won't blame me*, she told herself. But how could Kristine possibly understand the depth of Rikka's grief, her despair? Her concern would naturally be focused on the bereaved mother, her own daughter, Marianne, not Rikka. Not even Kristine could understand or sympathize with Rikka's suffering.

Mentz spoke to her kindly, gravely, but without empathy, attributing her mood not to spiritual suffering but physical weariness. Her mother watched her with helpless sympathy in her eyes. Rikka was too miserable to notice.

No one, so far as Rikka knew, ever spoke a word of blame about her. Yet Rikka's heightened sensitivity felt accusation in every glance, reproach in every word. Even a kindly remark from a neighbour woman seemed to hint at failure on her part. The tragic death of a child was not uncommon. But Rikka thought it must be gossiped up and down the coast. How strange and shocking a thing it was that Rikka, a most capable and careful mother, should have her niece's child sicken and die while in her care! It was that thought that haunted Rikka.

Could she have done more?

Would she have done more if Karl had been her own child?

Rikka remembered moments after Marianne had returned from America with her infant. She had ignored, almost snubbed her niece. She never fussed over Marianne's baby, never delighted in his giggles or held him just for the sheer pleasure of it. The other women had taken him to their hearts as all the babies of the family, indeed of the island, were loved and mothered. Rikka, worn down by her own children, resentful of Marianne's careless happiness, had almost refused to acknowledge little Karl. Had she withheld something from that helpless little child? Had some evil in her surfaced, something deeper than her conscious will? Had her failure to love the child as he deserved been the ultimate cause of his death?

If only her feelings had been warmer, more maternal, this cloud of doubt would never have blighted her mind.

But it was too late for that. None but God could know what culpability lay with her. No person but old Lotte could know how hard she had tried to save that baby's life. No one asked Lotte, or Rikka. Why would they? Stirring up that pain was like tearing off a scab to see a wound seep blood again. Babies died, none knew why, and women mourned and moved on. Maybe they felt it was a kindness to avoid the subject, allowing it to sink deep into that dark pond of Scandinavian reserve where miscarriages and sorrows and deaths were hidden but not forgotten.

And so, the weeks went by, and no one talked about what had happened. No one asked for details. Not even Marianne. Maybe she was simply unable to bear anything more than the stark fact of her child's death.

Because it was never discussed, Rikka never felt vindicated. Because she blamed herself, she felt permanently shrouded in suspicion that she may have neglected the child. Too dignified to moan and cry as some women might have done, she held herself aloof and carried on with her duties. Too proud to inflict on her family her dreadful tale of that day and night struggling to keep the baby breathing, she said nothing.

Never given an opportunity to be expunged, her self-doubt grew. A niggling voice whispered in her ear; *Maybe I was at fault. Maybe I did not watch the baby as closely as I should have. There must have been symptoms I missed. I allowed myself to be distracted because I did not care enough about Marianne's baby.*

No, she answered herself fiercely. *I did all that could be done. If it's God's will, it would have happened just the same - even if Marianne and Marmar had been here.*

Sometimes she almost believed it.

Meanwhile her compulsive anxiety about her own children grew. Her seventh child was born, a healthy baby boy, and Mentz named him Kristian in memory of her brother. Rikka thought of her brother often while nursing little Kris. The thought crossed her mind that she too was caught on the rocks, as her brother's ship had been, and no one heard her cries for help, or was able to help if they had heard. It seemed her spirit struggled drowning under an ocean of misery and guilt while everyone around her went on with their days as cheerfully as ever.

Mentz hired another man to help with the farm work, freeing up two of the young women to help in the house. Rikka observed wryly that he finally seemed to realize that, with Anna and other household servants gone, Lotte old and frail, and a new baby every year or two, Rikka's hands were full.

Coming into the kitchen one day she overheard him telling one, "Ingrid, I want you to take charge of the younger children. You see how pale Rikka is, how dark the circles are under her eyes. I want you to be ever at her right hand, do whatever needs to be done even before she asks."

Rikka turned on him fiercely. "What kind of mother do you imagine I am, that I would let a dairymaid look after my baby?" she railed.

She set Ingrid and Hanna to work cleaning out the children's room, washing the feather beds and pillows. There was indeed work enough for all of them, and she would nurse and care for her babies herself. With the older four - Ingeborg, Aksel, Asbjorne and Marie - in school most days, she kept Hjordis, Ruth and baby Kristian close by her side. She saw symptoms of a fever in every sneeze or sniffle. Her sleep was broken a dozen times a night as she started up from anxious dreams to listen for their breathing.

Marianne's baby had been buried in the churchyard cemetery, his grave marked by a stone carved like the stones placed years earlier for first his great-grandfather, then his grandfather and great-uncle. It seemed Marianne could not bear to return to her husband Ulf in Rorvik and leave that tiny grave. She stayed with her grandmother in the small house Marie had moved into after Kristine's departure. Rikka often saw Marianne walking up the hill to the graveyard behind the church, where she knelt by the little grave for hours. She never stopped to speak to Rikka. Ingeborg sometimes ran to walk hand in hand with her, but Marianne scarcely seemed aware of the other children.

Then one day Mentz came to Rikka grim-faced. "It is all over between Marianne and Ulf. Ulf came to see me. He says he can no longer bear having the baby's ghost come between him and his wife. He has asked the pastor in Rorvik to have their marriage annulled."

"What of Marianne? What will become of her?"

"I think she wanted this. Maybe she only married Ulf to give the child a father, and now she is glad to be done with him. She wants to board the *Marie* the next trip we make to Trondheim. She will take passage back to America. To Chicago."

"How can she do that? She has nothing left, no money ..."

Mentz interrupted. "We will pay her fare, you and I. I have already told her so. It's all we can do for her now."

Rikka stepped impulsively towards him to take him in her arms as she used to, when the comfort of her touch was all that was needed to soothe any worry.

He had already turned away and was gone out the door.

Chapter 10

Vikna, 1899

Before the century ended, North America had claimed most of Mentz and Rikka's extended family and many of their neighbours. The islands seemed to have turned themselves inside out in their eagerness to fill the ships steaming off across the Atlantic.

It was now three years since Marianne had left the island for the second and last time. Rikka's children looked forward to her letters as instalments of a modern-day saga. Chicago was a magical name to them, a place filled with adventure. Thirteen-year-old Aksel and twelve-year-old Asbjorne listened with shining eyes as Mentz read aloud Marianne's vivid account of Buffalo Bill's Wild West Show. Indians! Mustangs! Rough riders! Aksel's heart ached to see the great bison herds, which Marianne wrote had been hunted almost to extinction. Asbjorne was fascinated by her account of the native American encampment that accompanied Buffalo Bill to Chicago. Ingeborg, barely a year older than Aksel but a decade older in manner, quietly picked up the clippings Marianne had stuffed into the envelope. Rikka smiled to see that her daughter pinned on the curtain over her bed the crumpled newspaper illustration of a young woman holding a long-barrelled rifle. Annie Oakley had become Ingeborg's heroine. *No harm in her dreaming,* Rikka thought fondly. *God willing, she will never shoot a gun. Or visit America's wild west, either.*

But she reminded Gyda, the children's governess/tutor, to choose with care the reading material she gave Ingeborg, and to avoid novels that emphasized the sensational. No need to feed her frontier fantasies.

It was for Kristine's letters that Rikka watched. Kristine, Odin and their dozen children had experienced a few rocky years as newcomers in Minnesota, but that had passed. Having survived deceitful land agents, prairie fires, tornadoes, and disappointments, they still held high hope for better times. Those times seemed to have come. Odin along with Kristine's grown sons from her first marriage, Harald and Arvor, had earned homesteads in Minnesota. Their letters were tales of hardship and wonder, optimism and humour, filled with all the strange happenings of pioneer life.

Maybe they deliberately glossed over the underlying deprivation and hard labour. In any case, their letters eased the grief the two women shared. Their mother Marie had quietly died in her sleep the previous winter. Her death came the same disastrous night that, unbeknownst to them, Mentz's pride and joy, the cod oil factory on Helligholmen, had burned to the ground. Mentz and Rikka had each grieved. Rikka could almost forgive Mentz for seeming more stricken by the loss of the factory than the death of her mother.

"After all," he reminded Rikka gently, "your mother had a good and long life. It is better that she has gone to her reward now than suffer this added misfortune with us. She has been spared that."

Rikka grudgingly acknowledged the truth of his words. Besides, she had always understood that Mentz's business relationship with her mother, first as her employee and then her partner, took precedence in his mind over familial ties of affection, strong as they had grown.

So it was that, for Rikka, correspondence with Kristine and Odin sustained the lifeblood of family. For Mentz, the letters painted a picture of boundless opportunity.

Mentz chafed at the limitations of their narrow rocky isle. The disastrous fire came close to ruining them financially. He was forced to sell most of their property to pay the creditors. Declaring that "None of those who have depended on my good name shall suffer," he had been able to sustain near bankruptcy without loss of face. Above all, he was determined that his family did not bear the brunt of this hardship.

Perhaps he was a little too anxious that Rikka and the children be unaffected by their changed circumstances. He avoided sharing the true state of their affairs with Rikka. She assumed that any financial problems were temporary. He spent long hours in the office at the store, calculating how to maintain both their family and their business. Rikka knew only that he was preoccupied with commercial interests at a time she needed him

Rikka noticed with an uneasy feeling in the pit of her stomach that he read and re-read the letters, both those from Kristine and Odin, and the shorter notes from Harald. Letters from other friends who had emigrated seemed to find their way onto the three-legged table by his rocking chair, too.

Anna and Andreas' sons Marius and Parelius had been Rikka's music students before they left for America. Marius still exchanged letters with Ingeborg and the boys, and his parents always remembered

Mentz and Rikka with a letter at Christmas. It seemed their homestead in Wisconsin was prospering, but Anna hinted that the boys were eager to venture further into the wilds of the great northwest. Rikka noted with concern that Mentz had quietly asked Aksel to bring him their schoolroom atlas, and after studying it had turned down corners on the pages that showed Wisconsin, Minnesota, the untamed Dakota Territory and the nearly blank British colony to the north.

Kristine wrote that she longed for a photograph of Mentz and Rikka's growing family. She had never seen three of their children, as Kris, Torolv and Gunhild were born after Kristine and her family had left. When a travelling photographer appeared in Rorvik one day as Mentz was picking up deliveries for the store, Mentz invited him to bring his camera to Karstenoya. Their baby daughter was to be baptized that Sunday and all the community would be there for the occasion.

Sunday saw the family brushed and polished and dressed in their Sunday best. That was no small feat, Rikka observed to Gyda, with a family of nine children ranging in age from 14-year-old Ingeborg to six-month old Gunhild, squirming in her baptismal finery.

It took several minutes to get them all arranged to the photographer's liking.

"Move the little girl to the other side," he said, his voice muffled, coming from under the black drapery covering the camera and himself. "Can't you make that little fellow - what's his name? Kris? Stand still? Now Kris, you must look only at me, do you hear? Not at the pigeons, not at the kittens, only at me!"

Finally, the photograph was taken, the camera dismantled and laid back in its box. Besides a large, framed photograph for the family great room, Rikka ordered smaller prints from the photographer to send to family and friends in America. There were so many of them.

* * *

A month later, when Mentz strode into the house waving the packet and shouting that the photographs had arrived, all the children as well as the governess, nursemaid, elderly cook, and kitchen helper gathered in the great room. It was the first time the children had ever seen representations of their own faces. The framed family portrait was passed from hand to hand as Rikka sank slowly into her chair with the packet of small cardboard prints. One dear face was missing. Rikka wondered what her mother would have thought of this family portrait - Mentz' stern almost harsh expression, her own weary eyes, the children's fresh young faces. She noted for the first time the suppressed anxiety in Ingeborg's face.

Why does Ingeborg look so worried? At that age, I only felt impatience to be allowed to grow up, sure I would do something amazing with my life. And I wonder - is Asbjorne quite well? Those dark circles under his eyes never go away, not a good sign. But will you look at Hjordis! Such a sturdy straightforward little soul, so much like her father. And that blessed baby, Gunhild, staring bright eyed as a little bird.

While the children and servants drifted back to their schoolwork or household tasks, Mentz pulled up a chair beside her and laid the framed photo in her lap.

"We have a fine family, Rikka. We should be proud of them."

Rikka nodded, although she disliked Mentz's choice of words. Pride was a sin. She feared pride. She felt that whenever she had indulged her delight in music, her position in the community, her fierce joy in Mentz's love, it had invited tragedy. If not sin, it tended in that direction. It was perhaps better to remain soberly conscious of the fragility of life and futility of human endeavours. One must never give voice to happiness. To admit aloud any feeling of satisfaction in the appearance or accomplishments of her children would tempt fate to bring them down.

"We have been blessed," was her pious response.

Mentz continued. "We have a fine well-grown family and have done well by them so far. Healthy, strong, handsome children, getting a fair education. They should be capable of becoming anything they want to be."

He had Rikka's full attention now. What did he mean, become anything they want to be? That had certainly not been her experience. She had learned to curb her aspirations and restrain her feelings. Was it sensible or even decent to expect more for their children?

Mentz followed his own train of thought. "I am afraid for them, Rikka. When I started here, even though I was just a boy working for your mother, I saw opportunities. We have tried most of those ideas. We expanded our business, built boats. No one had ever used pipes for irrigation here until I showed it could work. We purchased another island and put a cod oil processing plant on it. We bought a steamship to carry people and goods up and down the coast. And your mother gave her support to all our ventures."

Yes, and you named the ship for her instead of me. And our fine modern cod oil plant burned to the ground. And the islands have had to be sold.

But she only said, "You have done the best you could, Mentz. The fire was not your fault. Maybe it is God's will that we learn to make do with less than we have been accustomed to."

Mentz frowned and shook his head. "That is the way old people talk. But we are not old, Rikka. We are not ready to give up. It is time for us to think of moving ahead. The fact is, I can see nothing more we can do here. The herring fishery is failing. Some fishermen will never be able to pay their account with us. And with our store on Helligholmen gone…"

Rikka nodded. She knew that the loss of the cod oil plant and their second store preoccupied Mentz. But their business here on Vikna had operated for three generations. Everyone in the whole district of Namdalen liked and trusted Mentz. Their financial situation could not be so very bad, could it?

Icy fingers closed around her heart as she remembered other times she had listened with half an ear, when Mentz had declared he would rather sell everything than go into debt.

He had lit his pipe as he talked. Rikka waited, silent and afraid to follow where his reasoning was leading.

"Did you know that the herring harvest dropped by half this year? That means there is no money for the fishermen to pay us, so our own supplies must be reduced. It is a vicious cycle. As our stock decreases, our old customers drift away. And now with the government subsidizing public transportation, running the Hurtigruten line up and down the coast, the steamship service we provide is no longer needed. The exodus to the new world is taking our young people, so we have fewer and fewer customers. That means less money, therefore we cannot buy stock and so we lose more customers. So it goes, round and round. In the meantime, our children grow and very soon will need to find their own way in the world, earn their own living. A living that will get harder to earn every year. They need opportunities, but opportunities here shrink day by day."

"Maybe the older boys could apprentice at some trade in Kristiansund, we have connections, your relatives in Trondheim or Bodo ..."

"No, Rikka, it's no good. Any of my family who might be able to help have already left for America. That is where opportunity lies now. That is the only hope for our children's future, unless we want them to continue plodding the same dull worn path and never use their brains for anything other than how to stretch their income to put shoes on their children's feet."

"But to leave home ... to leave Karstenoya ..."

"Rikka, when I first met you, you talked of leaving this island. You dreamed of doing great things. Remember? Be that girl again, for me, for your children. Let's sell everything here and go to America. If you don't want to be a pioneer, we can settle in a city. We have connections in Chicago ..."

Rikka shook her head and held up her hand as though warding off evil.

"No! Not Chicago. I am sick of hearing Marianne brag about her exciting life there. I don't want our children growing up in that evil city. If we must go, we will go some place we can start fresh, not depend on family to help us."

"Yes," agreed Mentz, "We don't want to burden anyone. Well, there is land in abundance in Canada, Odin says. They are thinking of moving there themselves. If we work hard, in a few years our boys will be landowners and our daughters will have homes and families of their own. How does that sound to you?"

Rikka shook her head doubtfully, but he laughed and pulled her to her feet. She smiled despite her misgivings and said, "If you will give me time to prepare, if you will wait until the children are older and able to help, and IF you include me in all the plans ..."

"Yes and yes and yes! O come away with me, my love!" And he danced her around the room laughing.

I know you, Rikka thought, excitement mingled with fear. *You are always happiest working on some new project. But what if this should be another one that fails?*

Chapter 11

Vikna, 1900 – 1903

The first years of a new century invite change.

"Time to let go of old ways and grasp new ideas. We must seize every opportunity," Mentz declared with relish. New ideas excited him. Rikka thought she had never seen him so ready to laugh, so invigorated.

Looking back over their years together, she guessed what he must be feeling. He had always seemed to her confident and capable. Now she realized that had only been her childish perception. Mentz had been a lad barely 17 when he sailed from Trondheim into their lives. He had needed to adjust quickly to the ins and outs of their world, not only the work expected of him but the hidden structure of island and family politics. He sat at their table and slept under their roof with the constant awareness that he worked for them. Her mother was his employer, her brother his best friend, she his undeclared love - it could not have been easy. How he must have envied Kris his freedom to choose the adventurous life of a fisherman over the drab daily burden of managing the store. Not much wonder he had stubbornly refused to show his interest in her until she almost forced him to speak.

Then had followed the painful time after Kris and Arnold were swept away. She understood now that Mentz had felt dutybound to care for her family; all because of his love for her, while not claiming her until he felt sure he would be considered worthy. He had managed it all with honesty, integrity, even dignity.

Life has not been kind to him, Rikka thought, ashamed to remember how she had resented his generosity to Marianne. At least that was all in the past. *Time indeed for new ideas.* They were free to do as they chose with the old family business, established for a time that was past, for a place that had changed, for people who had moved on.

Rikka vowed she would never again give in to fear or jealousy.

The thought of leaving had been difficult for her to accept. Even as a young girl, when she dreamed of life as a concert pianist, Rikka never imagined home being any place other than Norway. Once again she had to put the needs of her family before personal desires. That was, after all, the only decent thing to do. Every Norwegian Lutheran child had imbibed that principal with her mother's milk.

She remembered again her teacher's words: "Spirit needs muscle."

Not just the muscle of flesh and bone but the muscle of a spirit inured to hardship and suffering. Surely, we have had enough of that to make us strong for this venture!

Mentz held true to his promise to discuss every aspect of their move with her until they came to agreement. He had finally insisted she sit down at his desk with him, study the account books and see the true state of their circumstances. It became clear even to Rikka that there was no longer a living here for them; they were becoming poorer year by year. To emigrate was the only option that gave hope for their children's future.

Rikka felt stronger and bolder than she had ever felt since her girlhood. Adventure beckoned and some of her old recklessness returned.

Mentz brought home maps and pamphlets for her and the children to study and he shared every nugget of information he came across. She treasured their newfound closeness. Almost as satisfying was the children's excitement. Each tried to outdo the next in bringing arcane or useful bits of information to family conferences, held almost every evening in the great room after the younger children had been packed off to bed. They might be late comers to the long line of men, women and children sailing from Norway's rugged coast, but no troop ever had more enthusiastic recruits.

First had been the difficulty of deciding where they should go. That whole exercise had an air of unreality about it, as though she and Mentz were playing a game of pretend with the children, imagining a life in some made-up place. A big map arrived in a packet of material Mentz requested from the Canadian immigration department. They spread it out on the scarred surface of the worktable, set the lamp in the middle and marked the places where their friends and family had settled. Odin and Kristine's large family, confident after their success in Minnesota, had succumbed to the lure of free land in the Canadian prairies.

"After all," Kristine had written, "the North-West Territories cannot be much different from Minnesota."

Rikka studied the map and exclaimed in surprise at how far these places were from the ocean.

"Where on earth do they get fish?" she wondered aloud, and then joined in her children's laughter.

"In America, everyone eats meat!" Aksel, their bookworm, informed her.

He went on to explain that if they went farther into the prairies, they might have to do as the Indians did and hunt buffalo. He had decided that Marianne must be mistaken in thinking the buffalo herds were gone. How could just a few hundred white hunters have destroyed massive herds that plains tribes had hunted for generations?

Rikka smiled at the lanky boy, already as tall as she. "Then it is good that we have big boys like you and Asbjorne to hunt for us."

She knew that his favoured source of information, penny dreadfuls translated from English or German into Norwegian, were several years out of date and written specifically to appeal to a boy's love of adventure. Mentz had already assured her they would be in no danger from raiding Indians or stampeding buffalo, as the latter had been hunted to extinction and the former confined to reservations. Rikka kept silent as Aksel astonished his younger siblings with the story of a confrontation between the North-West Mounted Police and an Indian chief. His eyes shone and his narrow face grew flushed with excitement.

Dear Aksel, he thinks this is all one huge adventure! Who knows, maybe my boys will become great hunters. It cannot be worse than risking their lives on the North Sea. At least I will not forever be in dread of storms and shipwrecks.

A clerk at the Canadian consul in Kristiania had advised Mentz to apply for a homestead in a Scandinavian immigrant community establishing itself near Winnipeg. At least, it looked near, but when they calculated the distance, they realized it would be more than one good day's drive by horse and buggy.

"Maybe the winter roads are good for sleighing, so we can all go into the city once in a while. Much better than here at Karstenoya," said Mentz. "Where you and the children are as good as imprisoned all winter."

Rikka, nodded, but doubts darted through her mind like a flock of sparrows. Do they even have roads there? None showed on the map, just railroads and a few thin lines between large towns and cities.

"How long is the rail journey, Mentz? You say we will disembark at Quebec. But only look how far that is from Winnipeg!"

"Don't you remember, Rikka? What Kristine wrote about their journey from Minnesota to the Northwest Territory? It was an easy journey to their homestead, a week by train and another two days by wagon. And that is hundreds of kilometres further west. Travelling from Quebec City to Winnipeg cannot be difficult. Anyway, a few days on the train will give you and the children a chance to rest after our ocean voyage. Think how interesting it will be to see so much of this new country."

Mentz's thoughts had moved on. "We will have a railcar packed full of all the supplies we need to get us started building our farm ..."

Mentz was as excited as the children at their prospects in the new country.

Rikka smiled to herself as she studied the map. The district Mentz had marked, the one recommended by the Canadian consul, was sandwiched between two large areas of blue. Lake Winnipeg. Lake Manitoba. She measured with her fingers, comparing distances. Yes, they would be closer to both those lakes than to this unknown city, Winnipeg. Fishing might be good in their new home, after all.

Choosing their destination turned out to be the easy part. In the following months, they had to decide how to get there, what they needed to pack, and what possessions to give away or sell. Who knew what they might need in the new world?

After discussing it with sailors and businessmen up and down the coast, Mentz decided they should take their own little coastal steamer to Trondheim. He had found a buyer there for the *Marie*. They would travel by merchant steamer across the North Sea to England. From there they could take passage for North America on one of the immigrant ships that sailed weekly from Liverpool.

"But others sailed from Bergen," objected Rikka.

"And when have we done what everyone else does? We will find our own way, a better way."

She laughed and agreed. She was glad to leave that to Mentz to manage. When they had begun planning their move, she had imagined their family was complete. After all, she was nearing forty years old, already past her best child-bearing years when their ninth child, Gunhild, was born. Her monthly bleeding had become sporadic and irregular. She believed the barren prologue to old age had begun. She was almost four months pregnant with Thorstein before she admitted to herself that their tenth child was on his way.

Mentz agreed that sailing to a foreign land with an infant was unthinkable. With a sense of reprieve, Rikka continued to prepare for their departure while seeing to the children's education and the daily needs of their large household. They would put off their departure until next spring, when the baby would be a year old,

There was so much to do. When Kristine and her family had emigrated, Rikka and her mother had helped them with their preparations. This time it was all up to her. Who else could or would do it? Rikka worked from dawn until long after the rest of the household retired for the night. She drove Ingeborg and the serving women almost as hard as she drove herself, sewing, mending, knitting, packing, sorting, counting and recounting. She tried to imagine every contingency, supposing it was possible to calculate the precise number of blankets, sheets, pots and bowls, socks and sweaters required. She packed all their warm winter clothes first, having heard stories of Canada's bitter winter weather. As she filled the last trunk, she bundled up her embroidered bunad and crammed it in. She had worn the traditional dress on her wedding day and for every major feast-day since. *Maybe one of my girls will want to be married in it. The colors would be so pretty on Ingeborg.*

At last, the day of departure came. Their trunks were labelled, locked, and loaded onboard the Marie. Everything they could not bring with them or sell had been given away. The governess had left to return to Bergen. The other men and women who had worked for them and alongside them for so many years would stay on until summer, when the new owner would take over the store. Their old farm manager had bought the land from Mentz and would continue farming it with his sons, quietly content to be at last a landowner in his own right.

Mentz, Rikka and all their children would leave at daybreak the next morning.

For this last night, the housekeeper had conspired with neighbours to honour them with a farewell feast. Although the young folks were giddy with excitement and there was much laughter from the children's table, the older crowd sat in near silence, almost shy with each other, as though the family were already strangers to them, no longer one of their close-knit village.

Pastor Knudsen spoke what seemed to be on all hearts that evening. "With your going, an era has ended. This town will no longer be the same place we have known. Go with God's blessing and ours, knowing that you take a bit of Norway with you wherever you go."

Chapter 12

La Parisienne to Montreal, June 1903

Rikka hugged the baby to her breast and gazed across grey-green water to a foreign shore. She moved without volition over a sea that lay deathly calm. Before her the land was shrouded in mist, utterly unlike the sharp gray crags of Norway. Rikka knew she would never go home nor see those cliffs again.

"Mama, Mama!"

Rikka awoke and sat bolt upright, knocking her head against the rough beams that supported the upper bunk. For a moment she panicked, disoriented by strange odours and a dull rumble. The relentless vibration filled her belly and head and made it impossible to think clearly.

Gunhild ... poor little one she needs me. Rikka reached over her sleeping baby and patted the little girl, murmuring reassurance. As the child grasped her sleeve and slipped back into sleep, Rikka tucked the coarse blanket around her and tried to wriggle into a less uncomfortable position on the thin mattress. Her back ached, her arm had gone numb, her stomach grumbled.

We boarded the vessel a week ago and I do not think I have had an hour's stillness in that week. The older children are restless and excited, the younger ones need constant attention, and now everyone has this nasty sickness. Everything stinks of chamber pots, unwashed bodies and vomit. And garlic!

She had promised herself that she would keep a brave and cheerful mien during the trying journey, for the children's sake. When she saw the cabin on board *La Parisienne*, she made no comment about grimy floors or stained mattresses but went to work making it as comfortable as possible. When they stood in line with other passengers for their plate of greyish stew and she noticed Aksel and Asbjorne exchange grimaces as they poked through the mess, searching in vain for a portion of stringy pork, she gently urged them to eat up. When Marie, Hjordis and Ruth begged her to let them run about on deck, she merely told Ingeborg to stay close to her sisters and keep away from other passengers. This was as much for Ingeborg's safety as theirs. Rikka had seen how some of the men leered at Ingeborg and heard them speak to her. Their tone, if not the words, could not be misunderstood.

Even innocent Ingeborg sensed these were people to be avoided. Although she responded with a smile and a soft "God-morgen" to the tipped hat or greetings of some, she ignored with icy dignity the rude eyes and voices of others. Rikka wondered how her daughter had acquired such discernment almost overnight, after having lived her entire 18 years in the sheltered familiarity of their island community, where she knew almost everyone and everyone knew her. Now she was surrounded by strangers.

For the first time in Rikka's life, she felt disoriented and fearful. Even worse than the foreignness of their circumstances was the horrible feeling of being treated as a foreigner. The captain and crew spoke French and some English, the rest of the passengers spoke some other foreign language. Mentz called them Galicians. She could communicate with none of them.

For two full days after leaving Liverpool, she held her tongue, squared her shoulders and set her lips in a firm line. However, another unsuccessful attempt to get Kris, Torolf and Gunhild to eat the unfamiliar food broke her resolve. Hugging baby Thorstein to her breast, she vented her frustration on Mentz.

"Why oh why did we have to board a vessel filled with these Galicians? I suppose the captain feels he must bow to their wishes, there are so many of them. And it saves his own costs by having one of their number fill in as cook for us second-class passengers. But they soak everything in garlic! Maybe to cover up the smell of this half-rotten meat."

Mentz too seemed to have reached the end of his patience. It was futile to change anything now, surely Rikka must know that.

"Do you imagine I was asked to approve the passenger list before paying for our tickets? You know we agreed on this. The captain gave us a reduced rate since most of our children are so young. And he charged no passage at all for the baby. Do not complain, Henrikka."

And Rikka had not complained again. *He never ever calls me Henrikka!* Instead, she had prayed for more patience. *And a cheerful heart*, she added grimly.

Maybe God only heard the first request.

Mentz at least seemed mollified when she spoke approvingly of the captain, whom Mentz trusted. "Such a courteous man, he always bows and greets us when Ingeborg and I walk on deck."

Although I understand hardly a word he says. She suppressed a panicky feeling that fluttered into her chest and caught her throat. This would be only the beginning of not understanding, not being understood. From now on, she realized, she would always be surrounded by strangers, people she not only did not know but could never know because they had no common language.

But hold tight, only two more days, Mentz says, and we will be in Canada. A new land. A new life.

As soon as it was light, Rikka readied the baby and Gunhild, then took them up to the first deck. It was cold, but at least the air felt fresh and clean against her face after the squalor below. Mentz appeared, followed by their three younger boys, always early risers.

Rikka never heard him complain aloud, but she guessed by the heaviness around his eyes and the firm lines drawn tight about his whiskered lips that he felt appalled at their living conditions. Five years ago, Kristine had written to them a lively account of the crossing her family had made to New York. It had sounded eventful but not catastrophic. Rikka had prepared herself for something similar. Mentz had told the children to welcome any discomfort as an adventure. Remembering his hearty words, Rikka felt a certain grim satisfaction knowing that he suffered, knowing that although their choice of ships had been limited, he felt responsible for the choice.

She recalled all her first doubts about leaving. Over time her enthusiasm had grown, fired by Mentz's optimism and the children's excitement, but Rikka now convinced herself that she was an unwilling participant in the whole venture. Nausea and discomfort frothed into resentment and self-pity.

He is to blame! He never should have bought those islands, invested in the cod oil refinery. The old family business would have provided our living if only he had been satisfied. If only, if only …

She felt tricked into a journey she never would have chosen, but for Mentz.

Mentz returned with Kris, Torolf and Thorstein, now washed, rosy and eager to chase after the Galician children playing tag on the deck. Rikka busied herself fastening little Gunhild's pinafore and did not look up from her seat on a bench sheltered from the wind. She could feel his anxiety as he stood beside her. Finally, she relented and forced a wry smile.

"So. Our adventure begins with smelly diapers and pails of vomit. Indians and stampeding buffalo will hold no terrors for us after this!"

Mentz grinned, and relaxed the tension in his shoulders, stretching his arms and flexing his back.

"Soon this will be over. When we land, we can begin building our new life."

By now Rikka realized they had more than bad food and sea sickness to contend with. She noticed a young Galician woman rocking her fretful child, and, motherly instincts overcoming her diffidence, Rikka approached her to offer a sympathetic smile and a cup of water. The blanket fell aside, revealing a small face blotched red and hot with fever. Dread flooded her heart. *The children have played together, we share the same toilets, we eat the same food. Fevers like this will spread.*

When the ship docked at a rocky island in the St. Lawrence days later, and the passengers were ordered to assemble, her heart sank. The stern-faced little doctor on duty at the immigration centre came aboard and they lined up as directed. Rikka watched as he put his stethoscope to each chest in turn. Her consternation grew as he peered down the children's throats and checked their temperatures. Gunhild wailed as he jabbed a finger into her soft belly. He barked a short order in French to the white-veiled nurse who accompanied him. Rikka attempted to read the notes the nurse scribbled beside their names in the ledger. *What is she writing?* She tried out the few French phrases she had acquired on the passage.

"Bien? Tres bien?" she indicated the children, addressing herself to the doctor with what she hoped was a confident smile.

He shook his head, "Non, non, Madame." He delivered a volley of words that set her head spinning. Mentz left to fetch the captain, who hurriedly gave them to understand that the doctor suspected infectious disease among the passengers. Rikka could not argue with that. The signs were everywhere, in Torolf's feverish flush, in Gunhild's red and bumpy tongue. They would be confined to hospital under quarantine until this immigration official decided they posed no risk to the general population.

Rikka watched in despair as Mentz attempted to argue the ineffectual case that, while others might be sick, his family was only tired from the journey. All they needed was a bath, a clean bed, and a good meal at some inn. She felt ashamed that they could not make themselves understood. It humiliated her that they had no friend to speak for them. She tugged at his sleeve, and quietly urged him to make some arrangement to have their luggage unloaded and put in storage in a safe place. They would go to the hospital as the doctor insisted. Surely pretending to go of their own free will was more dignified than arguing and creating a scene. After all, they were strangers and aliens in this land.

By late afternoon, Mentz, Rikka and all ten children had squeezed into a closed wagon at Grosse Isle, each with a small satchel of belongings, all they were allowed to bring with them. A half hour later, Sisters of Mercy met them at the gate, and like brisk angels in their flowing white robes, ushered them into the stark clean corridors of the hospital.

Chapter 13

Grosse Isle, Quebec, Canada,1903

In later years, Rikka would never talk about those days in Quebec.

They arrived at Grosse Isle on June 27. If all had gone according to Mentz's carefully laid out plans, they would have acquired their settler's supplies and boarded the train bound for Winnipeg before the end of the month. A journey of more than a thousand miles would take at most two weeks.

"We should be at our homestead, ready to begin building our new home, well before the end of July," Mentz had assured his family. "That is still mid-summer, even in the northern plains of America."

"Measles," the immigration doctor wrote on some of their charts. "Scarlet fever" he wrote on others. Superintendent Martineau declared that *La Parisienne* was a hotbed of pestilence. The entire ship and all the luggage had to be fumigated. Mentz and Rikka's family, along with the other passengers, were confined to the quarantine station on Grosse Isle. Any showing symptoms of illness were sent to the quarantine hospital. That number included Rikka, Mentz and all ten of their children.

Those first few days passed like a dream for Rikka. Suddenly released from the misery of their onboard accommodations, freed from the constant stench and nauseating vibration, able to sip clean water and keep food in her stomach, her older children suddenly taken from her care, something gave way inside her. She fell asleep cradling baby Thorstein in her arms, waking only when he woke, sleeping when he slept.

Rikka woke one morning feeling once more alert and purposeful. A calendar hung below a picture of the Virgin Mary informed her that today was June 30. *What? Three days in Canada! Where is Mentz? How are the children?* She dressed quickly in an unfamiliar dressing gown worn thin with washing that had been left draped over the wooden chair beside her bed, and taking care to not wake the other mothers with nursing babies, slipped out of the small ward. She glanced back at baby Thorstein asleep and sucking his thumb, but decided it was better to let him sleep rather than risk waking him and others by picking him up.

Only her youngest had been left with her, the others dispersed to wards divided by age and sex. Following a birdlike babble of female voices, Rikka easily located the ward reserved for women. There she found Ingeborg, seated between the cots occupied by Marie and Hjordis. She greeted them as she would have in a normal morning at home in Norway, with smiles and hugs, hiding her consternation at the angry red welts covering Marie's round little face and extending down her neck to her belly. Both Marie and Hjordis were feverish and cross. Rikka was grateful that Ingeborg at least seemed well. Calm and helpful as always, Ingeborg soothed and amused her sisters. Rikka did not feel the need to stay with them long.

Next was the children's ward, where the younger boys and girls were housed together in a long room lined with small beds and white curtained windows. She spent more time there. Rikka was worried about little Gunhild, who had never before been separated from her mother. Gunhild held up her arms and silently begged to be held. She sighed and whimpered as she nestled against her mother's neck. Seven-year-old Ruth complained loudly that she wanted to go with "the big girls" and stay in the same ward as her sisters. Torolf tossed and turned on his little cot, seeming both fretful and listless. Kris was sitting up in bed scrutinizing an elephant in a picture book. From his bright eyes and cheerful greeting, pointing out to her the novelty of electric lights - "Mama, do you know, the light stays on all night!" - Rikka knew he had regained his usual high spirits. Only Gunhild seemed sicker, her fever worse.

Rikka accosted a nurse she found bustling down the hall carrying a bed pan. The nursing sister frowned and replied in French to Rikka's query, then scurried away, presumably to empty the pan, and returned a few moments later with a younger novice she had recruited to act as interpreter. Rikka recognised the language the younger woman spoke as English but could understand only a few words.

Remembering that when they had first entered this big brick building, Mentz with Asbjorne and Aksel had been directed to another floor, she turned and ran down the corridor to the staircase leading to the next floor. The men's ward must be up there. She had to find Mentz.

"Mentz! Mentz! Where are you?"

A familiar figure appeared at the same time the matron exploded from her office. She launched into an arm-waving tirade as she hurried Rikka and Mentz up the stairs to a common area on the rooftop. Rikka breathed in the fresh air and looked around, amazed. The hospital and quarantine station stood perched on a rocky island, bare except for a scattering of large solid very official-looking buildings. She had never seen a prison but thought this must be what a prison looked like.

The younger nurse had followed close behind them and now smiled apologetically as she tried to translate the matron's words into English for Rikka and Mentz. She glanced over her shoulder at the nursing sister who stood guard in the doorway with her arms folded in her apron, scowling at them.

"Mentz, you must ask her for me. What is wrong with Gunhild? Why is she not getting better? How long are they going to keep us here?"

But the most they could learn from the scowling nurse and the nervous novice was that the doctor would decide their fate, and he was "tres occupe" and would get to them when he had time. Rikka knew with panicky certainty that she had no control over what happened. She could only wait and show a patience and calm she did not feel.

Mentz hugged her and picked up the valise he had brought with him to the hospital. "At least I have some good news for you. The doctor made his rounds this morning and has signed the discharge papers for me and Aksel and Asbjorne."

"I must go now and check on our supplies and find a place for us to stay while we wait for our little invalids to recover. It seems there are hotels here, built especially for situations like ours.

Hopefully the little ones can recover quickly. God willing, we'll soon be on our way to the homestead."

Before the end of the day, Ingeborg and Marie joined their brothers at the boarding house. Mischievous seven-year-old Kris was declared by an exasperated nurse to be in fine health as well. She handed him the picture book to take with him as she shooed him out the door to join his father.

Now began the long frustrating wait for all of them. Rikka knew that Mentz thought constantly about work he should be completing on their homestead during these long summer days. It was inevitable that building their house and stocking up on winter supplies would be delayed. Each day lost cost them in lost resources, too, as their once seemingly ample funds were gobbled up.

"At least," Mentz said to Rikka, "The inn is close by and they speak English as well as French. The children and I, we learn more every day!"

As for the cost of the long hospitalization – well, he did not discuss those worries with Rikka. That did not stop her worrying.

The children were not entirely immune to the angst of their parents. Ingeborg declared on the second day in their third-class hotel that she could do all the work of the chambermaid and cook's helper, if their landlady would deduct her earnings from the board she charged.

Not to be outdone by their sister, Aksel and Asbjorne approached the landlord. "No one can chop or stack wood better than we do," Aksel claimed, in his fractured English. Since there was a never-ending demand for kindling to feed the wood stove in the high-ceilinged kitchen, the landlord smiled and nodded towards the gigantic woodpile.

That evening he remarked to Mentz that he had never seen two boys work harder.

"You will be in fine shape to cut wood for our winter fuel," Mentz told them. "In another few weeks we will be at our homestead."

This was not to be. What Rikka and Mentz had hoped would be only a formality, a few days lost in compliance with the stringent quarantine requirements imposed on newcomers, turned into weeks of isolation and inactivity for Rikka and the younger children. The calendar in Rikka's small room seemed to taunt her as it serenely marked time's irrevocable passage.

On August 6, Thorstein, Gunhild, Torolf, Ruth and Hjordis were finally declared free of measles, scarlet fever and any other lingering contagion. Rikka courteously thanked the ward sister and walked towards the door carrying Thorstein. Gunhild clung to her skirts, pale and quiet, and Torolf, Ruth and Hjordis followed close behind each carrying their little satchels. They walked out into bright mid-summer sunshine, wearing the same clothing they had on the morning the ship had docked almost six weeks earlier.

Summer would be almost gone by the time they reached their destination. Teulon, Manitoba. 1200 miles away.

Rikka prayed they would have time to prepare for the long hard prairie winter.

Chapter 14

Manitoba, 1903

They had been told that their homestead would be in the municipality of Rockwood in the province of Manitoba.

They left the tilled fields and lush orchards, the steepled churches and neat villages, of Quebec and Ontario behind. For long days they gazed out smudged windows, feeling as smudged and soot-streaked themselves, while the train chugged past craggy shorelines and through spruce forests. It seemed inevitable that they should end up in a place that was all rock and wood. Rockwood. There was nothing else.

When they finally pulled into the frontier city of Winnipeg, whistle tooting and smokestack billowing a cloud of steam over the platform, it seemed a different world. The sheer number of people at the Immigration Hall alarmed Rikka.

"Stay close by me," she ordered her children. She herself hung on to Gunhild's little hand and clutched baby Thorstein close. With a stern look and nod of her head she gave Ingeborg to understand that she was not to allow her little brothers and sisters to wander away. It seemed that every country she had ever heard of or read about was represented here in this drafty echoing building. As they had at the port of Quebec, they waited in line, but this time hoping for reassurance from an indifferent officialdom that at last their journey was nearly over.

Finally, it was Mentz's turn to enter the office where a suited and bearded gentleman presided over stacks of files. Rikka waited anxiously, the minutes creeping over her like the bedbugs onboard the ship.

Mentz returned from his consultation looking worried and upset. He informed Rikka there was no helping it, they had to spend another four, maybe five days here to obtain the required documentation for their homestead.

"Government officials are the same everywhere," Mentz grumbled. "They think theirs is the only business that matters."

"At least," Rikka said, determined to bring a smile back to his face, "accommodations are free!" The ten-foot by twelve-foot room allocated to their family seemed luxurious after the cramped seating on the train. Rikka set to work arranging their beds and putting the two younger children down for a much-needed nap. Free at last, Kris and Torolf escaped the room and went scampering through the hallways looking for adventure.

Ingeborg and Hjordis found them playing tag with a blond round-faced boy. This little boy also had sisters watching over him, as blond and round-faced as he was.

"God eftermiddag," the sisters greeted them.

Ingeborg and Hjordis looked at each other and laughed aloud. Finally, someone spoke to them intelligently, in words that made sense! Questions spilled out, they both talked at once in their eagerness to become acquainted with these wonderful beings. The Swedish sisters Inga and Elsa were the first people the girls had met since leaving Norway who spoke a language they understood.

With a trio of little boys and their new-found friends in tow, the girls hurried to share this prize with their parents. Rikka wept with relief. Here at last were people like them, people whose customs and manners made sense to her. Their accent and some of their words might sound strange, but she embraced the girls as though they were long lost relatives.

Inga and Elsa seemed to feel the same way. Faces wreathed in smiles, they cooed over baby Thorstein, admired the hardanger embroidery on Rikka's cap and exclaimed over Ingeborg's braided crown of glossy hair.

"Come with us!" Inga urged, tugging Rikka's hand. "Mama will be so glad to meet you. It is wonderful, you will be our neighbours at Rockwood! Tomorrow our brother is coming to take us to his homestead there."

Mentz brought along the map the immigration officer had given him showing his allotted quarter section outlined in blue. Soon he and the sisters' father, Ole, were standing with heads together, studying the map and deciphering the unfamiliar legend. They concluded that their farms would be four miles apart.

"But distance means nothing in this country," Ole assured Mentz heartily. "Lars says folks think nothing of travelling five miles to church. That's eight kilometers!"

When Mentz inquired about the location of the church, Ole replied that no church building had yet been built.

"But a church is the people of God, not the building," Ole declared. "Lars says the members take it in turn hosting services, and the elders of the congregation lead worship. You must come, too."

Mentz and Rikka soon learned that "Lars says" was a common refrain in this family. Lars, the eldest son and pride of his parents, had emigrated from Sweden three years previously, taken a homestead, broken the required acres, built a barn and a house. After harvesting a bumper crop of barley and oats he had sent for his parents and sisters and little brother to join him. They would all live together in the house Lars had built – "a fine sturdy house, from wood he cut on his own land" – and expand their farm from there.

After talking with them for the happiest hour in weeks, they promised to meet again in Rockwood. Ole's family would be leaving the very next day. Ole suggested Mentz send a telegram to the station at Teulon to let him know when they would arrive there. He and Lars would help Mentz transport his family and their goods from the siding to their assigned homestead. His offer was gratefully accepted.

Rikka's elation at meeting people like themselves was dampened somewhat by the realization that their own circumstances stood in stark contrast to the situation of their new friends. Rikka had no ready-built house, Mentz no established farm waiting for him. They had no community of family and church eager to welcome them. They had no barn stocked with hay and oxen, no root-cellar filled with potatoes and rutabagas.

What they did have was a family of too many small children and too few adults. They had a quarter section of wilderness and could hope for only a few weeks of good weather before winter began to close in.

"And we have new friends," Rikka reminded herself and Mentz with fierce gladness. "The Lord knew we needed help. He has given us good neighbours."

Finally, the last forms signed, the last tickets paid for, they boarded the train for the last time. It would be a short journey. The station master assured them it was only a few hours from the large CNR station on Portage Avenue to the little boxcar siding called Teulon. They looked forward to meeting the wonderful Lars with his team of draft horses and big wagon. Ole had also promised to arrange for them the purchase of a team of oxen and a milk cow.

As expected, a blond giant greeted them at the station. Sporting a weather-beaten hat set at a rakish angle atop his shaggy curls, he leapt from the wagon almost as soon as the train ground to a halt. His handshake was firm, Mentz noted with approval, and he bowed to Rikka with fine old country courtesy. His broad welcoming smile took in all the family. Maybe no one but Rikka noticed that his gaze lingered a little longer and his smile grew a little brighter when he spoke to Ingeborg. Rikka wondered if his sisters might have been playing matchmaker. Elsa had been so admiring of Ingeborg's long chestnut hair, her fine dark eyes. Might they not have described her beauty to Lars, just as they had described their brother's many fine qualities to Ingeborg?

Almost as though he had read her thoughts, Lars turned to her.

"Inga and Elsa begged to come with me, but of course I told them that would defeat the purpose of coming at all. There will be just room for you and your trunks in the wagon."

As he and Aksel swung the largest pieces of luggage into place, he explained to Mentz that Ole would be arriving shortly with the oxcart to carry the rest of their supplies – the canvas and ropes, the axes and building tools, the barrels of flour and cases of dried foods, and the fine sturdy stove. The stove was in Rikka's eyes by far the most important item they had bought. She knew it must serve for both heating and cooking in their yet-to-be-built house and would have to fulfill the same purpose for the meantime in their temporary camp.

"Papa and Mama want me to tell you, you must come to our place – my farm – for the church service on Sunday," said Lars to Mentz. "At the potluck dinner afterwards, you can meet all your neighbours. We can plan your house-raising bee."

Ingeborg looked at him with such open admiration that Rikka's heart lurched. *Oh, I remember, I know what she feels. Once I felt that way, too.*

Ole arrived with the ox cart. They all helped load the rest of their worldly possessions, the children cramming things into the wagon as soon as they were unloaded from the boxcar to the platform. They could hardly contain their excitement at finally heading down the trail, over rocky hillsides into scrubby bush – into the wilderness. Mentz took Torolf and Kris to ride with him and Ole in the oxcart, while the rest clambered into the wagon, perching on boxes and trunks. Rikka and the baby sat on the front seat beside Lars. The afternoon sun warmed their shoulders and carried a delicious odour from the surrounding meadow. Lars told them it was the smell of sweet grass.

"It grows wild along the trail. No good for anything, but the Indians like it and I don't know, I guess they use it for their heathen ceremonies."

Heathen or not, I like the smell, thought Rikka, but only said aloud, "I hope you will have time to teach us about this land, Lars. There is so much for us to learn. What are good berries we could pick? And who might sell us some chickens?"

Lars pointed out cranberry bushes and other unfamiliar bushes that he said might still have some berries. He explained that the season was past for other fruit bearing shrubs. Turning to Aksel and Asbjorne he said they must come hunting ducks and geese with him, as soon as he had finished his harvest. He would show them how to set snares for rabbits, too. He warned them that before anything else, they must begin cutting lumber for their house, and at the same time build up a good stock of firewood. A big woodpile was essential.

"Cut all you would need for a winter in the old country and then cut that much more. You have never seen winters as long and hard as they are here."

Rikka shivered in spite of the afternoon sun.

The days passed quickly, with sunlit hours never quite long enough for all they had to do. Aksel, Asbjorne and Mentz chopped down trees and brought them to their building site. Lars had pointed out the best site, a rocky knoll that he said would never be flooded, a danger they had not considered but now realized would be a fact of life in this country. Apparently, the whole area could become a floodplain if an ice jam happened to block the river's northward flowing. On the other hand, the nearby creek posed no danger, and would supply their household and livestock with ample water all year round.

Mentz seemed invigorated, eager to expend his pent-up energy after the long weeks of enforced inactivity. *Never happier than when starting a new project*, Rikka repeated to herself, smiling. This was no doubt the biggest project of his life. His high spirits were infectious. Rikka felt her own spirits rising to meet his. The new land, the fine late summer weather, the pervasive twittering and quacking and chattering of birds, inspired hope.

The dozen families who made up the little Baptist congregation warmly welcomed Mentz and Rikka and their family. Over a dinner of fried chicken and dumplings, with Lars' mother Gerta as hostess, the women shared with Rikka a bewildering plethora of advice about pioneer housekeeping. When one of the women asked Rikka whether any of her grown-up children might want to be included in the baptismal service, Rikka serenely replied that she, Mentz and her children had all been baptized as babies and accepted salvation as God's pure gift. No one commented, but a few of the women exchanged I-told-you-so glances. Rikka resumed her conversation with Gerta and resolved to avoid dissension. Differences might arise, but hopefully Christian forbearance and their neighbours' innate kindliness would prevent any falling-out. Even the discovery that her newfound Baptist friends deplored what they considered the legalism of her beloved Norwegian Lutheran Church could not dampen her happiness.

She and Mentz agreed on the slow oxcart drive back to their camp that they would support the Baptist congregation in every way they could. Pietistic Lutherans or Evangelical Baptists, what did God care? Minor aberrations in doctrine could never come between true believers. God remained God even though human interpretations might vary.

In any case, friendship and community counted for more than points of doctrine, especially with a house to be built before winter. The men of the congregation had been unanimous in their promise of a work bee, "as soon as the crop is off."

A log lean-to covered with a canvas tarp was their only home for the next few weeks. Aksel and Asbjorne slept in the wagon wrapped in blankets with a cowhide draped over them, pretending it was a buffalo hide and they were Indians. The girls and Rikka picked buckets of berries and spread them to dry in any sunny spot they could find, setting Torolf and Kris the task of keeping away birds and mice. Before the end of September Mentz and the boys had the foundation levelled, cellar dug and lined with stones, logs cut and stacked. Mentz had always loved building and regarded himself no slouch as a carpenter, but Rikka urged him to heed the advice of their neighbours.

"If we follow their ways now, they will see how we respect them and that we value their help," she whispered as they snuggled under heavy wool blankets while the children slept. "Time enough in the next year or two for you to build us a house as fine as the one we left at Karstenoya."

One morning she awoke to find frost on their blankets and ice in the wash basin. *Already winter is coming.*

Not all the men who had promised their help came, but those who did knew well what they had come to do. It took more than a few days and all the stones and logs they had prepared, with the children chinking uneven spaces and Ingeborg and Hjordis helping Rikka prepare gallons of coffee and pails of stew to fuel the work-crew. The walls grew, the roof beams were hoisted into place, a stone chimney built. Finally, Lars, who came early and stayed late every day, said to Ingeborg, who seemed to always find reason to admire the section of building he was working on, "You can tell your mother that we will move the stove inside now. No more cooking outdoors for you girls."

As the chimney pipes were wired up and hammered into place, Rikka paced off the room. There was the corner for the stove and the table next to it, along with makeshift shelves proudly fashioned by Aksel and Asbjorne nailed to the wall. The floor was made of rough-hewn logs, a trapdoor covering the opening to the cellar. The house was built a little taller than the Rockwood men had intended, but when Mentz pointed out that they needed the space for a loft, as they had somehow to find sleeping space for twelve people, they had smiled and nodded in agreement.

But even with the extra space for the loft it was a pitiful small house compared to the fine big home they had left in Karstenoya.

That was the house where I was born. All our children were born there. Once, I thought I would live in that house forever. Always warm and safe, always bustling with activity. Our family plus nine other souls ate at my table every evening the year round. And forty or fifty in the great room on Christmas and special days! A loft where we women did all the spinning and weaving, a dairy where the girls made butter and cheese, the out-buildings where the farm workers slept. Now everything must be done within these four walls. By our own hands.

Rikka looked around at her neighbours, Ole, Lars and the other men who had worked so generously. Her eyes filled with tears of gratitude and weariness.

"I do not know how to thank you enough for all you have done for us."

A big family such as theirs might prosper in future years, when they learned the ways of the land and when Aksel and Asbjorne were men.

But that time was not yet come.

Chapter 15

Teulon, 1903

Rikka thought she had never seen Aksel look happier. Thin face ruddy with exertion, he leaned on his axe and flexed his ropy arms. He motioned with his head to the growing pile of firewood that Asbjorne was stacking and grinned at her. She loved watching her boys. They worked as a team, they always had, perfectly attuned to each other. *Like a duet played by master musicians.* She returned his smile, nodded her approval, and turned back to her own chores.

Neither Aksel nor Asbjorne had "filled out", as her mother would have put it, but no doubt their lanky adolescent frames had grown stronger week by week. Aksel seemed taller, Asbjorne moved with greater confidence. *They will be fine men*, Rikka thought. A memory of her brother at that age flashed through her mind. Although it was 25 years since Kristian and Arnold had drowned, the thought of that day still made the breath catch in her throat.

But no time for looking back. Each new day brought new challenges and every night they fell into bed bone-weary but satisfied. The fine dry fall weather lifted their spirits. The robust cheerfulness of their neighbours encouraged them. Despite their inauspicious beginning in Canada, the visible success of other pioneer farms gave them hope that all would be well for them, too. Already their rough little cabin felt like home, Rikka thought, and the children seemed to be settling in. The girls had each found their niche, Marie taking charge of the baby while Hjordis and Ruth managed the younger siblings – Kris, Torolf and Gunhild – like a miniature work crew. They gathered sticks for kindling, carried water for the house or little pails of mud from the creek for Ingeborg, who covered her glossy braids with a scarf, mixed the mud with ash as Lars had shown her, and set herself to the task of chinking. Mentz was immensely proud of her. Rikka felt only baffled and amazed. What was going on with Ingeborg?

Rikka could no longer see in Ingeborg the pleasing child, the dainty girl, the obedient and dependable eldest daughter. Where had this new Ingeborg sprung from? The Canadian Ingeborg revealed a will of steel beneath her placid demeanor. She calmly set herself to jobs that in Norway would have been done by workmen and she firmly declined the mothering role now adopted by Ruth and Hjordis. Mentz smiled fondly and cheered her on. Rikka was reminded that Mentz had once shown the same dangerous indulgence to Marianne.

In a rare moment alone with him, she remarked, "Ingeborg needs to spend more time helping me prepare food for winter, instead of trying to learn men's work. It is hardly decent. And my two hands are not enough for all that needs to be done."

Mentz replied with a mirthless laugh. "Yes, I agree, we all have more work than our two hands can do. We both miss the men and women who used to share our work and our household. Haven't you noticed? Everyone here works at tasks they would not have done in the old country. School teachers plough fields and women who once directed a large household do the work of farmhands. Ingeborg is adapting to new ways, learning what she needs to know. But she is your daughter as well as mine, you must ask her to help you. She is a grown woman now. She will decide."

Ingeborg agreed reluctantly to help her mother indoors. "When I have time." That is, when she had finished chinking the logs and helping the boys haul the winter's supply of firewood.

Rikka realized that others besides Mentz approved of Ingeborg's unusual choices. Aksel and Asbjorne, who had always admired their big sister and deferred to her as the eldest and most clever, now looked to her as their leader. The fact that the wonderful Lars shared their admiration for their sister elevated her even higher. Throughout the fine weeks of September and October, Lars was a frequent and welcome visitor at the homestead, always bringing a useful tool or bit of needful advice or a helping hand. If Ingeborg had transformed the brother's duet to a trio, Lars had become the conductor of their music.

When Ingeborg decided that she must learn how to harness and drive the oxen, Lars seemed only too pleased to show her. When Ingeborg expressed a desire to help with the logging, Lars offered to teach her as well as Asbjorne and Aksel. When the boys reminded him of his promise to take them goose hunting, they all assumed that Ingeborg would be one of the party.

As Rikka once again set an extra plate for Lars at their makeshift table, she wondered whether he may have been the one to suggest these enterprises. *It's almost as though he is grooming her to become his helper.*

Before the end of October, something happened after church one Sunday that confirmed this not too unwelcome but still alarming thought.

The Sunday worship services that moved from one Baptist home to the next had been a Godsend to the family. The services offered them a ready-made community of believers and an opportunity to meet neighbours as well as providing friendships and fun for the whole family. The Swedish Baptist congregation anchored this Scandinavian settlement, just as the old parish church had been the focal point of Vikna. While adjusting to the quirks and vagaries of land and weather, it was comforting to find refuge in the familiar rituals of prayer, gospel reading and hymns. To Rikka, differences in doctrine were like variations in dialect, something to be respected and accepted. These folks were Swedish Baptist, she was Norwegian Lutheran. The Lutheran doctrine she had been born to was as embedded in her soul as the seafood she had grown up on was implanted in her bones. To change one was as impossible as the other. End of story.

It seemed not everyone felt as she did.

The women were clustered around the table that almost filled the kitchen-end of the main floor of the two-room log house where this Sunday's service had been held. The men and most of the children, bellies comfortably full, had dispersed to enjoy the autumn sunshine in the house-yard. Tables cleared and the girls entrusted, as usual, with the job of washing up, the older women were at last free to sit down and have a quiet gossip in peace.

Gerta poured Rikka another cup of coffee and told her, with the air of one imparting exciting news, "Pastor Nord - you know, the evangelist from Winnipeg I told you about? - is coming specially for our baptismal service."

Gerta's daughters, Lars' sisters Inga and Elsa, would be among those baptized. Rikka thought she understood Gerta's excitement. Adult baptism in this church seemed to fill the same role as confirmation did among Lutherans; that is, served as a celebration of a young person's public statement of faith, and congregational welcome into the adult community of believers. She smiled in sympathy with Gerta's motherly delight and described to her their own confirmation celebrations two years ago for Ingeborg, and last year for Aksel and Asbjorne.

Gerta looked at her strangely and said in a low tone, "You do realize, don't you, my friend, that true baptism is needed to secure their salvation? Baptism of a believer? Infant baptism is only a promise made by the parents. It has no validity. Each soul must make that decision."

Remembering in time that she and Mentz had agreed to refrain from any discussion with their new friends over points of doctrine, Rikka merely nodded, smiled and replied, 'Well, if God has not changed His mind, neither have we."

Gerta's lips tightened and Rikka realized her remark may have sounded flippant.

Before she had time to remedy the impression, Gerta called across the room to the group of girls giggling together, "Ingeborg, my dear! Will you come here, please?"

Ingeborg came to stand smiling at Gerta.

"Won't you tell your mother what you told me, my dear? I am sure she will be as delighted as I am. And as happy as Lars is, too!"

Ingeborg seemed momentarily nonplussed. Then she took a deep breath, and said, "Mother, you know that we cannot hang on to our old traditions in this new land. I want to belong here. I want to become a member of this church. I have added my name to the list of those to be baptized next Sunday."

Rikka stifled an expression of surprise, and Ingeborg stood a little straighter. "I did not tell you before, Mama, because I knew you would not understand. Your body is here but your mind is still in the old country."

As she turned away, Rikka heard her say, "And you will never give up your old ways."

Gerta could not quite hide her satisfaction at Rikka's obvious distress.

"Oh, these children of ours, they do keep us on our toes, don't they? We were not at all surprised when Lars told us that dear Ingeborg had decided to obey the Lord's call. She is such a sweet girl, you can almost see the spirit of Jesus shining forth in her. Her baptism will make her truly one of our spiritual family. And," she continued, "we will be so happy to welcome her into our earthly family, too!"

Rikka stared into the woman's guileless blue eyes. *Was she, this Swedish Baptist woman, suggesting that Ingeborg might become her daughter-in-law? As though a second baptism somehow made her fit to marry Lars?* A stinging retort rose like a bubble in Rikka's throat. A memory of Lars stopped her. She had seen his blue eyes, so like his mother's, gazing with untarnished love at Ingeborg and she remembered how Ingeborg's face shone when she looked up from her work and saw that Lars' eyes were on her. She could not speak words that might cloud that love.

She also thought how very crowded and uncomfortable they were likely to be this winter with twelve people sharing a one-room cabin. She lowered her own eyes and said nothing.

So it was that before another month had gone by, after only three months' acquaintance, Rikka and Mentz's eldest daughter, their Ingeborg, their pride and joy, was engaged to a fine young Swedish Baptist farmer. She and Lars would be married on the first Sunday of the new year.

Mentz was quietly content and assumed that Rikka felt the same.

"After all, it is the perfect beginning for her in this new land. You can see how fond she is of Lars, and he of her. She will live near us, and we will see them often. You and I can give them a hand when there is need."

Rikka wondered whether there ever would be need for them, with Ingeborg's mother-in-law the capable Gerta placidly managing the household and good-natured Ole ready to do the bidding of his wonderful son. She was quite sure that Ingeborg's life in the next few years would be much easier than her own.

Aksel and Asbjorne punched fists with a shout of triumph when they heard that Lars, their hero, would be their new brother. Marie turned almost demure as it dawned on her that after Ingeborg was married, she, Marie, almost fifteen years old, would become the young woman of the family. Hjordis accepted the situation with disdain and became even more of a tomboy. She promoted nine-year-old Ruth to become her deputy foreman over the small-fry work crew of Kris, Torolf and little Gunhild as they gathered a growing pile of kindling from the woods surrounding their little cabin.

Determined to at least make their first Christmas in the new land an occasion to remember, on rainy days Rikka set the youngsters to work helping her make candles in the lean-to beside their log cabin. With their cash running low she decided to save where she could while still maintaining traditions. *I am so glad I brought the moulds and candleholders from home. Christmas would not be Christmas without candles on the tree.*

"We will have the best Christmas ever!" she declared to Hjordis and Ingeborg. They grinned. She said the same thing every year.

The girls had helped with Christmas baking at home in Karstenoya but never under such cramped conditions or with such limited supplies as they had now. Instead of a pantry filled with square cheeses and blocks of butter and baskets of eggs, they hoarded the cream for a week to make enough butter for holiday cookies and cakes. Few ingredients were needed for some of the most delicate cookies, so Rikka gave the children free rein to make krumkake and rosettes as gifts for their new friends. Rikka's krumkake iron was in almost constant use. Crocks of pickled meats filled the lean-to and tins filled with flatbrod were stored in the dirt cellar, beside the bins of root vegetables given them by their neighbours.

"Will your family join us for Christmas Eve?" Rikka asked Lars one afternoon.

The fine weather had extended throughout a golden fall into December. Lars rode over to visit them almost every day, ostensibly to discuss something with Mentz or take the boys hunting. Sometimes, if there was no school, he brought his little brother Emil to play with Kris and Torolf.

"He begged and begged until I could not say no," he explained apologetically. Everyone smiled. They knew these were merely excuses for him to spend an hour or a minute with Ingeborg. As always, Ingeborg sat close to him on the wooden bench, and now added her voice to her mother's request.

"Oh, Lars, tell them they must come! Such wonderful celebrations we had back home in Norway, Mama playing the piano and all of us singing as we danced around the Christmas tree. Inga and Elsa and little Emil will love it!"

Lars nodded and smiled at Ingeborg with such love in his eyes that Rikka turned away. It was an alarming sensation, to know that soon her little girl would belong to another. *We must be sure to weld the connection between our family and his before they claim her entirely. Best set the tradition now – Christmas Eve with Ingeborg's family!*

Lars seemed to read her thoughts. "I know my family will be happy to come to share your first Christmas Eve here. Mama wants Ingeborg's family and mine to celebrate together – she ordered me to tell you we expect you all for dinner on Christmas Day." He savoured another bite of buttery roll. "Mama and the girls have been baking up a storm, just as you have. We will all be fat as pigs by New Years." He turned to Ingeborg with pretend consternation. "I will have to leave my suit-jacket unbuttoned like old Sven does. Will you still marry me with my belly hanging out?"

Rikka smiled as the teasing continued, with Ruth declaring she would take him, if Ingeborg backed out, and all of them agreeing that he would soon get his slim shape back if he had to subsist on Ingeborg's cooking. Regardless of their sparse furnishings and cramped conditions, this felt like home. Laughter and good company and friendship made all the difference. It would be a Christmas to remember.

The weather now turned bitterly cold. This was only a taste of things to come, Mentz said one morning, when he and the boys came in from caring for their few livestock. They had put up a rough log shelter in the fall to house the oxen, milk cows and chickens and to store their meagre supply of hay and grain. It was banked with snow and held enough warmth from the animals' body heat to get the hardy beasts through the coldest winter, but the flowing spring below the house had frozen over. The boys would have to chop holes in the ice and carry water for the animals as well as the house.

Aksel and Asbjorne came inside to warm their chapped hands at the stove. Rikka saw that their canvas pants and heavy boots were splashed wet and frozen.

"This will not do, boys. You must be more careful, we cannot have you getting sick!" Her words were scolding, and her voice was tight with motherly concern. Winter was only just beginning and already she could see it would be harder than her worst imagining.

Maybe it was for times like these, winters like this one, that God gave us Christmas. Advent, the time of preparation. Preparation for the time when light returns to the world, the darkest days are in the past and Christ is born. Hallelujah!

The last days of Advent sped by. She and Mentz missed seeing their new friends at Sunday services. The days were too cold and the distance too far for them to take the little ones out in the sluggish oxen-drawn sleigh. Ingeborg, Aksel, Asbjorne and Marie ventured out one Sunday on makeshift poplar-wood skis that Aksel had fashioned for them, and Lars continued his visits, keeping open the path from their homestead to the trail with his team and sleigh.

When Christmas Eve finally arrived, Rikka felt as excited as the children. The little ones perched on a trunk, keeping watch at the window through an opening they melted with their fingers in the thick layer of frost. Lars and his sisters arrived first, sleigh bells announcing their approach even before Torolf and Chris could see them. Gunhild scrambled down squealing, "Lars here, Lars here!" Ingeborg scooped her up and ran to open the door, spilling out lamplight and laughter as she greeted her lover and her friends.

Ole and Gerta arrived soon after with chubby little Emil bundled between them in the one-horse cutter.

"We wanted to leave room in the sleigh for Ingeborg and your girls to come home with our young folks," Gerta explained to Rikka as she unwound the mile of wool scarf protecting her head. "Since you are coming to our house tomorrow, Inga and Elsa thought it would be fun to have the whole evening together. And Lars says he wants to come tomorrow to fetch the rest of you."

She raised her hand to silence Rikka's response. "Now, no arguments! This is the best way. After all we are family now."

Gerta gave Rikka a hug. She smelled of cinnamon and snowflakes. Rikka remembered her mother and returned Gerta's hug.

The sweet soup of stewed dried fruits and spices simmered on the wood stove, platters of lefse and flatbrod waited on the table beside small trays of pickled meat and cheese and butter. Christmas Eve supper was a simple affair, Rikka having gratefully agreed to Gerta's insistence that they save their appetites for the feast she was preparing for the next day. *We could not serve a sit-down meal in this space anyway.* Rikka thought of the great room in their old home. *We used to serve more than thirty seated at table - and still had room for the Christmas tree!* She looked around the room, now cozily packed with young people. *But we sang the same blessing over our food ... I Jesu navn, Gar ve til bord ... What does it matter if Gunhild is stealing cookies off Lars' plate and the little boys are eating their third helping of sot suppe ... we are all family now!*

Mentz had agreed that there would be no room for the Christmas tree in the cabin until after they had finished the meal. Eager for the real festivities to begin, Emil, Kris, and Torolf helped Aksel and Asbjorne pull the table against the wall and arrange chairs for the 'old folks' on either side. Marie fetched the leather-bound family Bible from the shelf for her father and opened it to the second chapter of Luke, while Mentz beckoned to Lars to help him bring in the tree. Aksel and Asbjorne had spent hours tramping through the woods to find just the right one, not too tall but nicely shaped and fully branched. *Maybe too fully*, Rikka now thought, as she watched them squeeze it through the narrow doorway. As soon as it was in place, Rikka brought out the box of little candles she had made, and the weighted metal candle holders from their old home. The girls went to work fastening each candle securely to the branches. The little children sat mesmerized as Ingeborg helped Rikka light them. The effect was magical. Candlelight flickered on the polished copper pot, the frost-covered window, the children's upturned faces. It transformed their meagre surroundings into something gracious and touched with an otherworldly beauty. Mentz picked up the book. Every eye was turned to the glimmering candles and every ear tuned to his sonorous voice as he read the familiar old words telling the story they all knew so well, beginning "In the days of Caesar Augustus …"

"But Mary treasured up all these things and pondered them in her heart."

Mentz closed the book and looked up. The adults returned his smile, but the children were still transfixed by the tree.

"Gud Jul," he said softly, and Rikka began to sing. They all knew the old song. Every one of them, from oldest to youngest, had sung these words around the tree every year of their lives. *I am so glad, I am so glad, I am so glad it's Christmas Eve.* Mentz joined in, then Ingeborg and the older children and finally Lars and his parents and sisters. Lars held Ingeborg's hand and pulled her close to him. The little boys and Gudrun sprang from their seats on the floor, and after a few minutes of laughter and confusion, with Ruth's help they linked hands in a snug circle and walked slowly around the tree as they sang. *It feels almost like home.* A tear ran down Rikka's cheek and she bent to kiss baby Thorstein's downy head.

As they sang the last verse, Gerta began another carol, and their singing became less meditative, louder and merrier. One of the little ones danced close to Ingeborg, hugging her and laughing. It happened so quickly, they never after could remember clearly what occurred, but somehow Ingeborg's sleeve brushed against the lit candles.

In an instant she was aflame. "Mama! Mama!" and as she raised her arm the flames leaped to her hair. Help her someone help her and too many bodies moving all at once and all the wrong way so that when Lars shouted, "We must get her outside into the snow!" it seemed to take forever for them to get past the crying children and wrestle the screaming girl out the door. Rikka beat at the flames with her bare hands, but it was no use, it seemed as though the fire had gone through all the petticoats and layer upon layer of wool that they needed to wear just to keep warm and now it seemed impossible to get the layers away from her skin and when they finally succeeded the skin came too.

Chapter 16

Teulon, 1904 - 1905

Almost before they had the flames out and Mentz had carried Ingeborg back inside the cabin, Lars had re-harnessed his horse and leaped into the cutter. He galloped away into the darkness shouting, "Hang on, everyone! I will find the doctor and be right back."

But they waited in vain throughout the long night. As they feared, Doctor Neudorf had gone to spend Christmas with his parents in Winnipeg. The telegraph offices were closed. Lars roused the Teulon telegraph operator from his Christmas festivities to send an urgent message begging the doctor to return. The message was sent but sat unanswered for two days. Even the Winnipeg office was short-staffed for the holiday.

Lars returned by noon the next day bringing the best help he could find. Nurse Wickham was well-known to the homesteaders in the district, and if not well-loved, she was at least well-respected. She delivered babies and tended to broken bones and kept her nursing kit stocked for any emergency. Her patients did not always recover, but she had never been known to turn away anyone seeking her help. Her no-nonsense manner and preparedness more than made up for whatever may have been lacking in sympathy or expertise.

The little cabin that had been bustling with light and laughter just hours before now seemed frozen in silence. Mentz, Aksel, Asbjorne and Marie sat unspeaking, their eyes fixed on the quilt beneath which Ingeborg lay. Her breath came and went in short, ragged gasps and stifled moans. As the door opened, Mentz struggled to his feet and gripped Lars' extended hand.

Rikka rose from her chair by the bed and hurried towards them.

"Oh, finally you are here! But Lars, where is the doctor?"

Her lips moved but no words came as she listened to Lars explain that the doctor would arrive on the train from Winnipeg tomorrow or the next day. Until then, Nurse Wickham would take good care of their dear Ingeborg. His voice cracked as he asked Rikka, "How is she?"

"Out of her head with pain," Rikka answered tersely. She held herself rigidly erect, looking around the room, her eyes dark and ringed with sleeplessness. She summoned Marie to fetch food for Lars and the nurse. She sent Aksel to build up the fire in the stove, Asbjorne to bring in more wood. She set herself to making a fresh pot of coffee.

They tried to converse as they normally would, and not listen for the cries of pain coming from the curtained alcove. The nurse's voice was calm and compassionate as she murmured, "Sorry, dear girl, you must be brave. Just a little bit more, we must get all these bits of cloth out of your burns and let the good air cool them. This cloth soaked in vinegar will help."

Six pair of eyes turned pleadingly to the nurse when she emerged from behind the curtain. She smiled and said in a matter-of-fact tone, "I have given her a sleeping draught. It will bring some relief for the next few hours."

To Aksel and Asbjorne, she said, "I have an important job for you young men. You must take some pails and fill them with good clean snow. We will try to cool her burns."

She turned to Lars. "I think you had better send another telegram to Doctor Neudorf and tell him that I suggest he bring a good supply of morphine. Make sure he knows that the case is severe, the patient has burns over half her body."

Lars choked on his response, nodded mutely and hurried away. They listened as the squeak of sleigh runners on snow and the jingle of bells on the harness gradually faded. They fell back into silence.

Nurse Wickham accepted a cup of coffee from Rikka and sat beside her at the table. "I will stay here for the next few days, at least until the doctor comes. It might be better if the children could go and stay with friends for a time?"

Rikka shook her head. "Lars parents have already taken our youngest five, all except the baby, to stay with them. As for Aksel and Asbjorne, they would refuse to leave their sister. And Marie must stay to help with baby Thorstein."

The nurse stared at her. Rikka could almost see her counting. "Do you mean to say you have ten children?"

Rikka drew herself to her full height and looked down at the woman. "Yes. I have ten fine healthy children. Ingeborg is the eldest. We have never lost one."

Despite her stoic determination, the tears spilled over.

The doctor finally arrived and brought vials of morphine. It took almost a week for Ingeborg to die.

Each of them mourned in his or her own way. Rikka wrapped the putrid sores in strips of muslin and dressed the poor ravaged body in the fine double-shuttle woven wool dress that had been set aside for her daughter's wedding. Aksel and Asbjorne insisted they have a part in building her coffin. Mentz agreed and watched dry-eyed as they carved an inscription encircled with vines and flowers on the lid. Marie did a pen and ink drawing of their old home in Norway. Hjordis and Ruth cut locks of their hair and wrapped them in brown paper. Each of the younger ones brought a stone or pinecone to be tucked into the coffin beside her. Lars and the other men of their little congregation kept fires burning in the Baptist cemetery for three days to thaw the ground enough to dig the grave. When the coffin was at last lowered into the earth, Rikka felt that a part of each of them went with it.

"A beautiful service," Gerta said as she hugged Rikka. Rikka nodded but could not reply. Her every thought these days began, "What if …"

What if they had never left Norway? What if they had gone on another ship, and no one got sick? What if they had not been delayed in Quebec? What if they had arrived at their homestead in early summer? What if they had had time and resources to build a bigger house? What if Ingeborg had not met Lars, had not joined his church, had not promised to marry him … then that disastrous evening would never have occurred. Her family would be intact. What if what if what if …

Rikka could not bear to be long in the company of Lars' family. *Gerta means to be kind,* Rikka told herself, *and poor Lars seemed almost as broken as the rest of us.* But though his sisters Inga and Elsa cried copiously at the funeral, and Ole tried hard to retain an expression of solemn respect, their natural cheerfulness could not long be bound. Rikka knew that soon Ingeborg would become to them only a bittersweet memory, a tragic story to be told in hushed tones when the children were not by.

But it would never be like that for Rikka. Nor for Mentz.

Rikka hoped Marie and Hjordis, who had looked up to Ingeborg but had not shared the closeness they had with each other, would become too much occupied with the serious business of adolescence to dwell long on their sister's death. *Thank God that Gerta and Ole whisked the younger children away so quickly; they may not really understand all that happened, how Ingeborg suffered.* Ruth sometimes spoke of Ingeborg as though she were still with them. Kris, Torolf, and Gunhild already seemed to have become accustomed to her absence. They might never forget that night, but what they remembered of Ingeborg's injuries was blurred and indistinct.

As for Aksel and Asbjorne, they grieved for her as though all light had gone out of the sky.

It was for the sake of their children that Rikka and Mentz decided they must continue as members of the church community. They resumed going to the travelling services as soon as weather and time allowed. It became easier as months passed. Rikka felt if not pleasure at least a stirring of her former contentment to see Inga and Elsa tease a smile from Marie or Hjordis as they strolled by with linked arms, to see Aksel and Asbjorne lounging by the horse barn with a gaggle of boys. She tried not to think of Lars as unfaithful to Ingeborg when she noticed him bending over a pretty blond miss, the travelling pastor's daughter. She mentally shrugged when she overheard Gerta declaiming about the young lady's musical ability.

"Our girls just love her so much," Gerta gushed. "They are quite determined to adopt her into our family."

Rikka remembered when Gerta had praised Ingeborg in the same way and wondered how much Lars was influenced by his mother's fickle opinions.

I am glad at least that you will never know that heartbreak, my poor daughter, she thought.

What hurt her most was Lars' almost total neglect of Aksel and Asbjorne, who had in the few months of his courtship of Ingeborg come to regard him as their own mentor and friend. Their logging work continued almost daily, as Mentz planned to build a barn and add a room to their cabin as soon as weather and time allowed, but it had ceased being a joyous challenge. Without Lars working beside them and bereft of Ingeborg's cheerful heartening presence, the work was cold, hard, and lonely. The two boys and Mentz often came home weary and discouraged.

"It's a far cry from the way we did things in the old country," said Mentz to Rikka. "Remember how we would mark the trees in our woodlot, maybe one or two years before we planned to use them? And then mark them again before stacking them, so we would know exactly where each one should go? Yet here we are, hacking down trees we don't even know, hoping they will be fit to use." He continued in a jovial tone that, Rikka knew, cost him some effort. "But no matter. If it's not good for lumber, there is always a need for firewood. I hear there is a shortage in Winnipeg, they are buying up all they can get their hands on. If the boys have time to make a trip with the oxen to the siding, we could set aside a little cash to cover farm expenses this summer."

Rikka knew the cash was desperately needed. Although they seldom talked of it, the funds they had counted on to make a good start in this harsh land had dwindled to almost nothing. *The children are growing, they need shoes, warmer clothes. Aksel*

She scrutinized the boys as they sat wolfing down their supper. She knew it was never enough for their growing appetites. "You must have a hollow leg," she used to tease them. But the dark circles beneath Aksel's eyes, the hoarse cough that kept Asbjorne from sleep, were no joking matter.

"Do you think we should take the boys to see the doctor next time you make a trip to town?" she wondered aloud one evening. The bitter cold had relented, and the longer daylight of March lured the older children outside after supper for an hour of sliding on the snowy slope by the creek or checking on rabbit snares. It was a rare treat for her to have Mentz alone, with only little Thorstein and Gunhild playing together on the floor.

Mentz stretched his legs and smiled at her. "They are fine, Rikka. Their young bones are growing too fast for their muscle to catch up, that's all. As for Asbjorne's cough, well, I cough too. All that freezing cold air is hard on the lungs. It will clear up as soon as the weather is warmer."

The weather did grow warmer, in fits and starts. By May the snow was gone except for stubborn drifts deep in the woods. As the snow melted and the ground thawed, they discovered why Lars had advised them to build on the hilltop. The stony ground around their house soon dried, but the boggy land surrounding it did not. The girls discovered that when they drove the milk cows to the little meadow a quarter mile up the creek, they had to pick their way carefully and stay on the path.

"It seems the swamp gets deeper as the days get longer," Marie complained to her mother after she and Hjordis almost lost their boots in the sucking mud. "When I stepped off the path, I went right in over my knees."

"It's muskeg, that's what it is," Mentz said. His face was grim. "Ole told me that Lars says most of our land is muskeg. That's why it was available, why the land agent assigned it to us. No one else would take it."

"But – why didn't they tell us that? Why did no one warn us our land was no good?" Rikka felt stunned.

"I guess they thought it was none of their business." Mentz spoke wearily, his shoulders sagging. "When I talked to Ole that first day – you know, when we first met them in the immigration hall in Winnipeg? He asked a lot of questions and I told him about our old country business, the store and the farm and the steamship. I didn't want them to think we were destitute, like some immigrants. They probably thought we had the resources to handle a bit of bad land and could buy better land once we got settled."

Rikka felt such a welling-up of rage and disappointment that she turned to hide her face from Mentz. *We don't have other resources. Only this swampy land – and friends who care so little for us they won't even tell us the truth.*

She scarcely heard Mentz add, "And after Ingeborg – well, they didn't have the heart to tell us."

* * *

The girls became accustomed that summer to herding the cows home for milking every evening while walking barefoot on the trail. If they slipped, they ended up in the mud. Boots were too precious to risk losing in the swamp. The cows seemed content to plod through the muck, and on some parts of the trail, the girls walked almost level with the cows' backs. Everyone became accustomed to doing whatever had to be done, as dictated by season and weather. Life settled into a semblance of routine. The children learned to steal eggs from ducks' nests that spring and to keep a smudge fire burning in the yard all summer to discourage the hoards of mosquitoes. The boys snared rabbits for their stew pot and cut firewood to peddle to their neighbours. By fall they had earned enough to buy new boots. With their help, Mentz had cleared the brush and broken a small plot of land and planted a field of oats. Rikka and the younger children planted a garden, and Aksel cut stakes to weave a willow fence securing it from the predation of deer and chickens. They filled their root cellar with enough vegetables to last until the next year.

Another bitter winter settled on the land. *This time*, Rikka said to herself with grim satisfaction, *at least we know what to expect.*

They continued to attend the little Sunday gatherings when weather allowed, grateful for the fellowship, but politely declining another invitation to be re-baptized. Lars and the pretty daughter of the travelling Baptist preacher announced their engagement and Rikka's congratulations were almost sincere.

Mentz accepted the offer of work at the lumber mill for the winter, walking on snowshoes the two miles there and back each day. The boys, proud to be earning money also, went every day into the woods and came home in the early twilight plodding by the oxen with a load of wood on the sledge. Every week they made the long slow trip to the siding to deliver a load of firewood and brought home cash for Rikka to add to their savings hidden in a coffee tin.

"For the house," Asbjorne would say as he handed it to her.

"For your new coat," Aksel said as he gave her his share.

Asbjorne continued to cough every night, and now Aksel joined him. The muffled hacking chorus from the loft permeated the dreams of the family sleeping on their straw mattresses below. Rikka, too tired to add another worry to her nights, hardly heard them.

It was already past mid winter when Rikka noticed the rag Asbjorne carried with him every day was spotted with blood.

The money in the coffee tin was barely enough to pay for the doctor as well as the medicine he prescribed.

Asbjorne coughed his last on a raw day in March, 1905.

Aksel died a week later.

Chapter 17

Teulon, 1906-07

Rikka stood beside the open grave. Her eyes were dry and her voice steady as she repeated the familiar words in the old tongue that to her was the only language fit for speaking to God.

Faber var es ert i heminriki …

Our Father who art in Heaven …

The visiting pastor was both Norwegian and Lutheran, two unlikely blessings. They seemed to her paltry recompense for the Lord to provide, after all He had taken from them.

Rikka raised her head as the prayer ended and looked around at her remaining family. They stood beside the small coffin, all those who had loved Gunhild during her short life. Mentz held four-year-old Thorstein, who stared wide-eyed at the tears running down his father's bearded cheeks. Marie and Hjordis, both now as tall as their mother, had taken charge of the often rowdy but today subdued trio. Ruth,

Kris and Torolf stood silent and still. Rikka stifled the sob rising in her throat. *They look so frightened. They have seen two sisters and two brothers die. I must not let them see me break. Lord don't let them see me break. Help me teach them to think of Gunhild safe with Jesus, see her in Heaven welcomed by Ingeborg. And her brothers. Aksel. And Asbjorne*

Gunhild's illness had been sudden and brief. It had at first seemed nothing more than a common childhood upset, something to be set right with a spoonful of molasses and a day in bed. Vomiting, then diarrhea and a bit of fever. Rikka expected her to be her sunny little self by the next day.

But it turned out that she was not the only one affected, nor was this outbreak limited to children. First one and then another in their rural district were struck down, some only for a day, others emerging from their homes pale and thin after weeks of illness. A few hardy souls joked about it.

"Just a case of the trots, nothing to worry about, happens 'most every spring."

Dr. Neudorf looked worried. He drove around the district in his buggy visiting the sick. He took water samples from the creek and posted signs. "All drinking water must be boiled."

Soon most had recovered. For Gunhild, the boil water order came too late. She died a week after she first fell ill, only a month before her seventh birthday.

"At least she will not be alone," Lars remarked clumsily, patting Mentz on the shoulder. Their eyes turned to the small wooden crosses that marked Aksel and Asbjorne's graves. Mentz nodded, his face impassive, unmindful of the tears that continued to well from his stricken eyes.

Several from the Baptist congregation had come to show their sympathy for the bereaved, although Rikka and Mentz were no longer even nominal members. Sixteen months ago, when Aksel and Asbjorne had died, Rikka and Mentz had assumed they could be buried next to Ingeborg in the Baptist cemetery. It was Gerta who had been delegated to inform them that the cemetery was for baptized members only.

"And poor dear Ingeborg was a baptized member of our church. Whereas the rest of your family is not." Gerta had hurried on, avoiding Rikka's eyes. "But don't worry, there is that new cemetery, for the pioneer community, it will take anyone, it's not part of the church."

So Aksel and Asbjorne and Gunhild will lay forever separated from Ingeborg.

For Rikka, it was the final blow. She, and consequently Mentz and the children, left the fellowship of the Baptist congregation. The children did not complain. They were content to see their friends at the little country school they attended when weather and chores allowed. Mentz and Rikka continued their life-long Sunday rituals of scripture reading and prayer and hymn singing, the only difference being that now they worshipped as a family rather than in a community of believers.

The brief funeral over, the coffin lowered into the grave, hands shaken, and condolences whispered, the mourners drifted away a few at a time. Spring sunlight dappled the fresh green grass, a meadowlark sang from its perch on a fence post. Horse-drawn buggies trundled one by one down the trail away from the cemetery. Ole and Gerta's family were among the last to leave. Inga and Elsa hugged Hjordis and Marie. Rikka forced a smile as Lars and his young wife, whose name she somehow could never quite remember, approached her. The young woman handed Rikka a little bouquet of spring flowers tied with a blue ribbon and Lars said, "Gunhild was a favourite of mine, Rikka. Remember how she used to run to hug me when …"

He stopped. Rikka finished for him.

"When you were almost part of our family. Yes, I remember."

Gerta claimed Rikka's attention, enveloping her in one of her famous hugs. "Oh, how I have wept for you, my dear dear Rikka! Poor little Gunhild, she is safe with

Jesus now. Last Sunday at church we prayed for your family, each of you by name."

"Thank you, Gerta, thank you," Rikka murmured, extricating herself with some difficulty.

"We miss seeing you at Sunday service," Gerta continued. "Maybe you and Mentz and the children will join us for worship this summer? It would be good for you, help you move on from this sorrow…"

Move on! As if my children, my sweet babies, will be left behind and forgotten. Never, not by me!

Rikka merely shook her head. Even Gerta could see she was near tears.

"Oh my, I almost forgot."

Gerta reverted to her everyday matter-of-factness and handed Rikka a small cloth bag. "We picked up your mail for you when we went to the post office yesterday. I know you have not had time to get it."

Rikka took the bag and thankfully waved goodbye to their friends. She and Mentz and the children were finally alone in the graveyard except for two young neighbours who had volunteered as grave diggers and now waited for the family to leave so they could complete their task.

`On the way home she opened the bag. Two letters, one from her sister Kristine in that new province with the funny name – *how do you say Saskatchewan?* - and one from her niece Marianne in Chicago. Hjordis and Marie entertained the younger children in the back of the wagon with a singing game. Mentz was lost in sombre reflection. She opened the letter from Kristine.

She and Kristine had continued to correspond regularly, writing to each other at least every month all through the decade of their separation. Kristine's family had moved from their homestead in Minnesota to the Northwest Territories, as that part of of Canada was known in 1903, the same year Rikka and Mentz's family emigrated from Norway. In what seemed now like the distant past, Rikka recalled studying the map of Canada and feeling delighted to see that their destinations looked not very far apart. On the map they had seemed two adjoining territories. She had found the reality far different.

Both their families had seen changes. Kristine's family had secured good land and established farms and schools for themselves and their children in a territory that just last year was granted provincial status. Rikka's family, in the same years, had been devastated by disasters.

Rikka opened the letter and felt momentarily shocked by Kristine's merry greeting, then reminded herself that her sister could not have known about their most recent tragedy when she wrote this letter. They did not yet have telegraph service in Kristine's remote corner of the world. Rikka's own brief letter informing Kristine of Gunhild's death could be weeks getting to her sister. Loneliness overwhelmed her. She put the letter in her pocket to read later.

While Marie tucked Thorstein into his trundle bed and Hjordis, stockinged legs dangling from her favoured perch on a rafter, read a bedtime story to the other children in their loft bedroom, Rikka brought out both letters and handed one to Mentz. She read Kristine's letter and then waited while he finished Marianne's. He seemed to be reading it several times over, frowning as he did so. When he looked up, instead of handing her the letter he took her hand and said, "Rikka, we have something we must discuss."

"Marianne writes there is a big demand for skilled builders in Chicago. The city is growing, wages are good. She talked to Nils at church – you remember, I told you about Nils who has the construction company? my brother used to work for him. She told him we had not had good luck starting a farm here. And – well, you had better read for yourself what she writes."

He handed Rikka the letter, indicating a paragraph near the top of the second page.

"So, my dear Aunty Rikka and Uncle Mentz, this idea might be of interest to you.

Nils asked me to give you his address and suggest you write to him. He says he has heard about the building work you did at Vikna, and he needs men like you. He would have a job for you whenever you can come to the Windy City. I do not know what your situation is now, of course, maybe all is going swimmingly on your homestead in Manitoba. But if you want to make a fresh start and test the waters yourself, dear Mentz, before dragging Aunty and the children to a new home, I have room for you in my little house until you get settled."

The letter ended with love to all the children and "Tell little Gunhild thank you for her drawing of her kitten."

Rikka's tears overflowed. Silently she handed the letter back to him.

"Rikka, I think we must consider this offer."

Mentz spoke slowly and deliberately. Rikka knew he had for months been searching for some avenue of escape from this disastrous homestead. She wondered if he had, in fact, suggested such a scheme to Marianne in a private letter to her. The old jealousy she had struggled so long to keep hidden stirred to life. *Who was Marianne to suggest Mentz leave his family and come to her? Marianne who had never remarried, who earned her own living and bought her own house and had only herself to care for. How dare she try to steal Mentz?*

She bowed her head and closed her eyes as Mentz continued in his most gentle tone. "I know how hard this has been for you. I blame myself for bringing my family here. I cannot bear to see you suffer any more. If you agree, I could get ready during the summer, stock up enough wood and hay to last through the winter, then work at the mill here until Christmas to earn extra cash for my train fare. If I leave in the new year, you and the girls will be able to manage until I can send you some money."

With a sob that broke her heart, he added, "And finally we can get away from this cursed place."

It was shortly after Christmas when Mentz slung his duffle bag over his shoulder and kissed Rikka goodbye at the rail siding. The feeder line would take him to the big CPR station in Winnipeg. From there, he would take the Soo Line, the rail line that stretched all the way from Montreal to the west coast. Mentz would go from Winnipeg to the Twin Cities, change trains, then continue to Chicago. Sleeper cars and dining rooms were available for those who could afford them. Mentz planned to travel cheap. He paid only coach fare, sprawling on the same hard seat day or night, grabbing a few winks of sleep when he could.

By mid-January 1907 he had become one of the hoard of faceless workers trudging every day to labour on construction sites. Chicago was booming. The Chicago Tribune boasted that 1906 had been the most prosperous year the city had ever seen and 1907 was predicted to be even better. United States of America was on its way to becoming the leading industrial nation of the world. There was work for everyone. Marianne's friend Nils immediately hired him as one of a crew of builders constructing another office building. Sensing that Rikka disapproved of his friendship with Marianne, Mentz thanked Marianne for her kindness in offering him a room for a few nights but declined making it a permanent arrangement. He promised that yes, he would see her every Sunday, and found a rooming house for himself near the construction site.

Mentz discovered that, while wages sounded high, they were nowhere near as high as the cost of everything needed for daily life. This was no more profitable than eking out a subsistence on a Manitoba homestead, the only difference being that, instead of being misled by the vagaries of land and weather, now he was duped by an unknowable adversary. He had become a pawn in some game the rules of which he did not understand.

"It could be worse," he wrote to Rikka that spring. "I live cheap, share my room with a big Swede who works the night shift at the packing plant. He has the bed by day, I have it at night. We split the cost, and our landlady provides me with an evening meal in exchange for repairs to her house. I can put a bit in my bank account and send you a little, too. If we can just hang on a few more months, I will have enough saved for a new start."

Then another unforeseen event almost destroyed his last shred of confidence. In October of 1907, the American banking system ground to a near standstill. Panic among nervous investors followed rumours of bank failure, rumours that Mentz never heard. Alarmed depositors withdrew their money. When Mentz arrived at the bank where he had faithfully deposited half his weekly pay cheque, the doors were closed and barred. Stunned, he realized that his hard-won savings were gone. Adding to this blow was the news that many Chicago companies could not meet their payroll demands.

Unable to collect the wages owing him and having lost almost everything he had earned in the previous months, Mentz decided his only recourse was to continue working and have faith that some of the money owing him might eventually be paid.

Rikka's heart sank as she read his letter.

"Workers here have few rights. If an employer cannot pay, he will simply tell his workers to go home without their wages or offer a promissory note which may or may not prove good."

"I know my work is good, and my employer is a fair man. He was a newcomer himself, twenty years ago. He knows what that is like. He had a hard struggle building this company. I trust he will do right by me."

Rikka, miserable at the prospect of another season without Mentz, put the letter aside after reading it aloud to her children.

"Your father is too good. He trusts others to be as honest as he is himself. He may never get his money out of that bank, nor the wages owed him. What do we know? He may return home poorer than he left."

Hjordis was quick to protest. "Mama, he sends money to us, and that hasn't been lost. Aren't you proud of how well we are doing? And our neighbours are good to us. I think it is better to trust people than to suspect everyone of being dishonest."

Rikka bent and gave Hjordis a quick hug and exchanged a wry smile with Marie. The older girls had become her confidantes and sounding board as well as her helpers. She discussed everything with them and found her burdens seemed lighter when shared with them. But, she realized, she sometimes voiced thoughts that would have remained unspoken if Mentz were here.

It comforted her somewhat to know that at least Marie, the oldest of her surviving children, fully understood their need to be shrewd. Despite the pious platitudes voiced by many, and while respecting Mentz's unshakeable belief in the essential goodness of his fellowman, her innate scepticism had won out. She must not let the world continuously get the better of them.

This last year had, for her, been a forced march into financial acumen. By dint of thrift that bordered on parsimony and a sharp eye for a deal, Rikka had been able to add a few good milk cows to their farm. She trained her daughters in skills she herself had first learned as a girl and later mastered while overseeing the workers in their small household dairy in Norway. Marie and Hjordis learned quickly and, by mid-summer, housewives shopping at the general store in Teulon would watch for the day "those pretty Norwegian girls" brought their cheeses and slabs of sweet butter to town.

Rikka put Ruth and the three boys in charge of the chickenyard. To ensure that even the youngest made the logical connection between effort and reward, she allowed them to keep a portion of the egg money. The sheep, Rikka oversaw herself, grazing them in a movable paddock kept well removed from bramble thickets and mud holes, and locking them safely in the barn at night. She hired a sheep shearer in the spring and thereafter spent every fine summer evening sitting in the door yard at her spinning wheel. She and the girls would knit the fine woolen yarn into sweaters and socks and mittens for the long winter.

They grew another huge vegetable garden. Their pantry and root cellar were full. All of them, from five-year-old Thorstein to Rikka, spent long days cutting, loading, and stacking the winter's supply of firewood. They would not starve. They would not freeze. They would stay healthy and strong. They would get through another winter without Mentz.

"Mama, you haven't opened the other letter, the one from Auntie Kristine."

Hjordis shoved the envelope towards her mother. *It is strange how Hjordis seems to hunger for news of her aunt and cousins,* Rikka thought. *The girl was only seven the last time she saw them, yet she listens to every bit of news as I read Kristine's letters aloud. And then takes them away with her to read over again.*

Rikka felt a twinge of pain when she thought how separated her children had grown from any extended family. This was not the way she and Mentz had planned for them to grow up, with no solid church home, no secure place in the community. She supposed the children must have made some school friends during their sporadic attendance, but she rarely saw their neighbours. Hard weather, constant chores, difficult travelling had isolated them. The children were lonely. Memories of good times in Vikna and news of these cousins in far-off Saskatchewan must seem like a fairy tale to Hjordis.

Rikka opened the letter and began to read aloud all the usual assurances that "We at our house are well and hope my letter finds you and your children the same, dear sister."

Kristine's letters varied only in details, Rikka thought, always full of satisfaction over the successes of her grown children, celebrations of marriages and grandchildren born. Never a hint of worry, grateful for recovery from minor mishaps or illnesses, always expressing thankfulness at their seemingly blessed state. Rikka felt ashamed to write to her sister, since her own letters were so often by necessity a litany of sorrows. It seemed almost indecent to admit her own pain in the face of such unremitting contentment.

"How the Good Lord has blessed us!" Kristine wrote. "Our little congregation continues to meet every Sunday at one or another of our homes. We expect our church building will be finished before winter. It will even have a bell tower. Odin has been elected an elder, our grandchildren will grow up going to church school and learning their catechism in the church we have helped build."

Rikka read aloud mechanically, her thoughts wandering away from Hjordis' shining eyes and upturned face and her other children scattered about the crowded room in various attitudes of listening or inattention.

Kristine has put all our old sorrows behind her. Rikka wondered sometimes if her sister ever thought of the tragedies their family had borne. Of course, Kristine remembered, but not with the anguish that plagued Rikka. *Maybe,* Rikka thought, *it's my own recent troubles that keep the old grief alive inside me.*

Sometimes Rikka thought of Nils the pigherd and the stories that haunted her childhood. She shuddered at the memory of his words. "Ah you must look sharp, child, or the monsters will find you, wherever you are."

The monsters in his stories had always taken unexpected forms, a troll emerging suddenly from the quiet night or a raging storm-serpent rising out of calm weather. It was true. It had been so all her life, from her father's drowning to Gunhild's sudden illness. Disaster came in a new form each time, never with any warning.

You could only keep yourself strong and watch and wait.

"The spirit needs muscle."

The letter finished, she passed it into Hjordis' outstretched hand.

She looked at her own hands, spread her fingers wide and saw the cracked nails and hard calluses. These hands were no longer the strong, graceful fingers of the musician – she had not touched piano keys since leaving Norway more than four years ago. They certainly were not the nimble fingers of the proud young girl who had gloried in the praise of her scarlet-clad Queen. Her hands were not beautiful, nor very skilful, except for the drudgery of spinning and knitting and all the hard work of raising crops and animals and children. She doubted that she could do more than an adequate job of playing piano for an ordinary Sunday church service, the Samlingsang or doxology.

She now knew something that as a girl she had failed to fully understand. *The spirit needs more than the strength of the body. The spirit itself must grow muscle through hard use, just as the body grows muscle through practise.* She felt sure that her inner being, her spirit, must have grown tough and strong. She had been almost broken, seen her own children die, endured long bitter winters of loneliness and hardship. Nothing had destroyed her spirit. So long as she refused to give up, she was not defeated. She might still triumph from disaster, make her family proud, her children healthy and successful. They only must survive until Mentz earned enough to buy them another and better farm. She had to hang on and not give up. That was all.

If only Mentz would come back soon.

Chapter 18

Teulon,1908

"Without which I cannot live."

Mentz's words ran through Rikka's brain like a phrase of familiar music.

She slapped the reins lightly against the mare's flanks. The rhythmic beat of trotting hooves and the sibilance of sleigh runners on snow added a lively Mozart melody to the words. It was a rare moment of peace.

Rikka had insisted that no one accompany her on this maiden trip with their new outfit. After promising the younger children a treat from the Teulon general store and assuring the older ones they could have the horse and sleigh for the young people's social Friday evening, they acquiesced. It was a novel experience to travel alone and in such luxury. She felt pleased with her purchase, the first to stretch beyond bare necessity. When she and Mentz had arrived at their homestead five years ago, they might have deemed a team of horses to pull their wagon, sleigh or plough a necessity. They soon discovered that the meager earnings of the farm could not justify such a purchase. The slow, strong, easily kept oxen would have to do well enough. Besides, as Mentz often pointed out in their early days at Teulon, "We have nowhere to go in a hurry. And as for the farm work – why, the hooves of the oxen are better suited to our boggy land than the hooves of a horse."

But in his most recent letter from Chicago, he had encouraged her to buy the mare. He wrote that when he returned home in April, they must have a horse and buggy to travel to the best farm his savings could get them. Rikka had endured another winter without him. He had taken a second job, working in his off-hours for a friend of his boss, building an elaborate gazebo on the man's mansion grounds. It was a job that paid very well.

"Although it may end by costing me almost as much as I earn," he had written in what Rikka knew was meant to be a jocular tone, something to make the children smile. "You remember I told you in an earlier letter about this man's very large, very friendly, very foolish dog. I think it is a Saint Bernard. It is as big as a calf. The beast follows me around and watches me as I work. Yesterday, as I carried an armload of lumber, I tripped over him and took a nasty fall. I had to take the streetcar to my rooming house and stayed back from work today for the first time, since I cannot bear any weight on my injured leg. But I trust it will be better by tomorrow."

His letter had started out as usual, comments on the family news she had written him in her last letter and encouragement for her to use the funds he had sent her. As usual, he said little about his everyday life in Chicago, other than to relate the story of his ridiculous accident with the big dog. It was the ending of the letter that caused her heart to sing. Rather than just signing off as he always did with love to her and the children, he added a paragraph for her eyes only.

"You cannot know, my dear Rikka, how I long for you. In a few weeks we will be together again. I will sit by your side, content just to look at you, like that great foolish St. Bernard watches me. Maybe you will trip over me and order me out of your kitchen. But I will refuse, I can never again leave you. Do you remember when we first met, when you were no more than a child and I just a boy? I think I have loved you since that first day. Life has not always been kind to us. But nothing was too hard to bear with you by my side. You, my wife, my Rikka, you are the sunshine without which I cannot live."

Without which I cannot live.

Rikka repeated the words aloud. The mare's ears flicked back and forward again, alert and well-trained, as though she were asking, "What is your wish, my mistress?"

Rikka laughed aloud. It had been a long, long time since she had felt like laughing, really laughing, not a half-sardonic chuckle over some folly but laughter that bubbled up from an overflow of delight. She felt almost like a girl, remembering the warmth of Mentz's body next to hers, his strong arms around her. *It is not too late*, she thought. *Not too late to know desire or be desired. Not too late to show him how much I love him. Not too late to be happy.*

The smile was still on her lips as she drove past the livery stable, the blacksmith shop, and the hotel opposite the train station. Snowbanks piled high by winter winds had shrunk under the March sunlight and revealed the dirt and garbage that had lain concealed in them. Ice puddles pockmarked the rutted main street. It had been a long hard winter, one of the worst in memory, people said, but it would soon be over. While they heard stories of boxcars in Winnipeg being broken open by people desperate for fuel, she and her children had put by a woodpile that got them safely through the bitter months. Soon winter would be over, and Mentz would be home.

She stopped in front of the large frame building housing both the general store and post office. She clambered down from the sleigh, voluminous skirts gathered in one mittened hand, and looped the reins around the hitching post.

For a moment she felt surprised to see no other customers in the store. The town seemed uncommonly quiet until she recalled what day it was. *Monday! Of course. Most housewives, especially those in town, do their washing on Monday.*

Rikka had decreed long ago that one laundry day a month was sufficient for her family, as laundry 'day' actually consumed two days of hard labour. This was especially true during the winter when it involved breaking the ice to carry pails of water, heating tubs of water on the stove, scrubbing and rinsing and wringing, all by hand – and then another day or more dodging sheets and towels and shirts and petticoats as they dried on pegs and racks after being brought in from the clothesline, frozen solid.

Some day, after Mentz is home and we have a better place, I too will have a weekly laundry day. She smiled to think that even the drudgery of washday could be seen as a privilege.

She observed with a twinge of annoyance that the woman behind the counter was not the genial storekeeper nor his soft-spoken wife but their part-time helper, a ferret-faced young woman who seemed to take malicious delight in speaking too rapidly for newcomers to follow. English was the language of school as well as business, so Rikka's children had adapted quickly. For Rikka, it was a struggle. This young woman, who possessed the unpronounceable name of Georgia, seemed to delight in humiliating her on the infrequent occasions Rikka entered the store unaccompanied by one of her youngsters.

"Good afternoon." Rikka decided it was safest to speak first, to set a dignified but courteous tone. "I have come to buy from you a few yards of that cloth which you sold my neighbour, Mrs. Yonson."

"I am sorry, what did you say? I am sure I don't know any Mrs. **Yonson,**" the woman replied, grinning smugly from behind the counter. "Could you possibly mean Mrs. **Johnson**?"

Rikka ignored her smirk. "I will take three yards of that material and two of the blue flannel."

"And" she added impulsively, "a few of those apples."

The apple barrel in a cool corner by the window was almost empty, but even the withered apples on the bottom looked delicious. Her children had not had any fruit since Christmas; it would be a wonderful treat.

With her purchases wrapped in brown paper and totalled, she rummaged in her purse for the coins, keeping a sternly noncommittal expression as she read the sum pencilled on the bill, but thankful that she had not also asked for the flour or sugar she had intended to get. *The girls will just have to use their dairy money to get it when they deliver butter on Saturday.*

She realized Georgia was speaking and turned to her an inquiring face. The girl sighed with exasperation and repeated in a loud slow tone, as though speaking to one impaired in hearing or intellect, "You - must - sign - for - your - telegram."

Rikka stared at her. *What telegram?*

"But we had our mail already. Marie brought it home. Only a few days ago."

Georgia shrugged. "Well, this must have come after she picked up your mail. We wondered why no one came to get it. I guess it could not be anything very important."

"A telegram? Not important? Is that not for me to decide?" Rikka grimaced. She had never, until now, received a telegram. Only dire circumstances could necessitate sending one.

"Yor-yee-ah! Why did someone not come to my farm with it?"

Georgia glared back at her. "There were no instructions about delivering it right away! And it says right here, in the telegraph company book, that agents do not have to deliver anything more than a mile from the office.

She slammed the ledger down on the counter. "If you immigrants want to live way out in the bush – what can you expect?"

Rikka carefully signed her name in the ledger with shaking hands and ripped open the pale-yellow envelope. Painfully, slowly she deciphered the English words.

"Dear Aunt. Mentz died last night. Letter to follow. Marianne"

Rikka read it again. The words made no sense. Mentz? dead? When his loving words from his last letter still echoed in her mind? It must be some horrible mistake. Marianne had heard about his little accident, that was it, and impulsive as always, she had assumed the worst and sent this tragic message.

Rikka found the date. Friday, March 6, 1908. And today was March 9. Surely, Marianne would have sent another message by now to explain the mistake?

"Is that all?" Rikka's tone was harsh. "Is there not another telegram? Another one that came after this?"

Georgia seemed to have no difficulty understanding her this time. She excused herself and hurried to the back of the store, returning in a few minutes with the storekeeper. Suspenders slipping over his fat shoulders, Rikka pictured him as she had glimpsed him at other times, dozing in the great armchair in the office where he sorted and distributed the mail. When he saw Rikka's face, his own took on an expression of commiseration.

"Ah there now Missus, there now, you've had a shock, you have, some bad news no doubt. Best sit down for a minute …"

Rikka interrupted him. "Please, I must know if another telegram has come for me? Or perhaps a letter?"

"No, no nothing more has come." He shook his head.

"But" he continued, his voice dripping with kindness, "Why don't I just run over to the telegraph office and see if anything came today?"

"I will go with you." Still clutching the yellow paper, Rikka hurried after him.

There was no second telegram. With the now-conciliatory help of the storekeeper and telegraph operator, Rikka composed a return message to Marianne. Her purse was almost empty. She recalled, as though from the distant past, the brown paper parcel containing her purchases. It must still lie where she had left it on the store counter. She showed the storekeeper the bill. Although not quite enough to cover the cost of the telegram, he handed over payment and said he trusted her to make it good.

She returned to her sleigh, shook the reins, and retraced the rutted trail she had travelled only an hour before. Somehow, she must get home, back to the children, before she let herself fully understand. She must keep telling herself, it is a mistake, a terrible mistake. Mentz's words echoed in her mind, but instead of a Mozart melody they seemed like the sombre refrain of a Bach concerto.

Without which I cannot live.

Clouds driven by a sharp north wind lowered the sky almost to the treetops. Bits of hard dry snow pelted the mare's brown back and settled in Rikka's graying hair.

The next afternoon, the horse-drawn sleigh was again on the snow-packed trail to Teulon, this time with Marie and Hjordis crowded onto the front-seat beside Rikka. It was a silent journey. Ruth and the three boys huddled under a cowhide robe on jump-seats in the back. Although Thorstein hardly had a clear memory of Mentz, he had built up in his mind heroic images of his father. Rikka could hear him whispering questions.

"Ruth, if the angels took father to heaven, they will bring him back again, won't they?"

Ruth's answer was kind, if not quite in line with Lutheran theology.

"Angels don't bring people back to earth once they've gone to Heaven, Thorstein. I guess they don't want to leave. But their souls come back to visit us sometimes. No, not ghosts! Like Ingeborg. You're too little, you don't remember her, but sometimes she comes to me in a dream. And then next day I find a ribbon I thought I'd lost or see something beautiful that I know she would have liked. And I know it wasn't just a dream, she's here, even though I can't see her."

Rikka heard Kris choke back a sob and wondered whether she should hand the reins to Hjordis and reach back to give him a hug. Instead, she began to sing.

"Praise to the Lord, the Almighty, the King of Creation ..."

The girls joined in and then the boys, even little Thorstein. They sang one hymn after another, their voices blending in three-part harmony, only falling silent as they came to the town.

The telegram response from Marianne awaited them at the store.

Mentz's accident, tripping over the big dog, had broken a bone in his leg. The resulting infection caused his death. His burial would be on March 10. *Today is March 10.*

Sick, dead, buried, before I knew anything.

Marianne's letter the next week explained more fully but did nothing to ease the pain or to quell Rikka's rising desperation. Marianne wrote that Mentz had been unwell all winter but had only worked all the harder, as though afraid of running out of time. When he was injured, he downplayed its seriousness and refused to ask for help. His landlady at the rooming house called a doctor and insisted he be moved. The doctor shook his head, saying that bones weakened by tuberculosis become infected easily. Gangrene had already set in. He finally notified Marianne. As soon as she saw his condition, she ordered a cab and took him to her house. There she cared for him with "all love and attention" until his death.

"I would have telegraphed you as soon as I learned of his injury, dear Aunty, but he forbade it. You must understand how quickly everything happened. I called another doctor, who would have performed an amputation if Mentz had agreed. Sepsis already had him in its fatal grip. He made me promise not to contact you, as he still believed, somehow, he would be cured. 'If I die, time enough when I am gone to alarm her. I cannot bear to cause her more grief.'"

Rikka read and reread the letter, imagining each step of the tragic episode, telling herself, *It would have been different if I had been there. He should not have taken that extra work, he must have been so tired, worn out with heavy labour. I know he did it for me and the children. And he would not call a doctor, he would pretend the injury was less than it was, wanting to avoid extra expense. All this while writing to me to go ahead and buy the horse and sleigh!*

Could she have prevented this? *Yes,* she told herself fiercely, needing to blame someone. *If I had been stronger and managed better, he would not have felt the need to work so hard, maybe would have taken more care of his own well-being. If I had prayed harder, more sincerely. It is my fault. God is punishing me.*

Next her thoughts turned to Marianne. Only thirty-five, middle-aged for a woman, but Marianne had always been a beautiful and vivacious person, even as a girl, and no doubt had kept her looks. She had not worn herself ragged on land that was surely cursed, nor borne and buried so many children as Rikka. It must have been a pleasure to Mentz to be cared for by such a person, someone he loved. Because he had loved Marianne, just as Marianne had loved him. Rikka felt she had always known it.

How mad I was not to have seen it all before! Of course, he wanted to be with her.

Not with me. He would have come home if he had really loved me, would have worked in the stone quarry as some of the men in Teulon do, or gone to the big lake and fished like the Icelandic communities north of us.

Her thoughts went round and round like a dog chasing its tail, sometimes blaming herself, sometimes raging at Marianne, sometimes at Mentz, sometimes at God. She went about her days mechanically, hardly noticing how Torolf lingered by her side, scarcely hearing Marie tell the latest news from town. Life had to go on, but it went on without her awareness. Neighbours came, bringing a ham or a loaf of fresh bread and their sincere condolences. She tried to be gracious but could hardly choke out more than a few words of thanks. She wished drearily for some place to hide, away from the stricken eyes of her children or the prying eyes of neighbours.

More letters came, from Marianne, with the money Mentz had entrusted with her for his family, and from his employer, with the wages he had been unable to pay Mentz before his death.

"If I can be of any help to you or your family, now or in the future, do not hesitate to contact me."

Rikka dropped the letter carelessly into the kindling box by the stove. Marie retrieved it and tucked it into her handkerchief box for safe keeping.

Letters of sympathy came from Kristine and the other family members Marianne had contacted. Rikka wrote to no one.

Finally, months after Mentz had died, a letter arrived from Saskatchewan that seemed to wake Rikka from her stupor. She studied the letter silently for several minutes before reading it aloud to the children as they crowded around the supper table.

Kristine wrote, "My dear sister, Odin and I want you to come to us. Move your family to Saskatchewan. You must leave all the sadness you have endured in that place and make a fresh start, for the sake of your children. We will gladly welcome you into our home."

Rikka had to stop reading because tears at long last threatened to spill over, and because of the hubbub that arose around the table.

"Hurrah! We can go on the train!"

"Does this mean we will see our cousins?"

And from Hjordis, "Oh Mama! How wonderful it would be to see Aunty Kristine!"

Rikka smiled for the first time in weeks as her eyes skimmed the next lines. She felt an overwhelming surge of gratitude for her sister, who knew her so well despite their long separation. Kristine understood Rikka's pride, and even while offering it she knew that Rikka would reject outright charity. Her letter went on to explain that they knew of a farmer, a widower, a man of good character, who needed a housekeeper for himself and his two children.

"If you prefer, he will provide a home for you and your children, in exchange for managing his household. Your older children might help as needed on the farm. The younger ones can attend school. His farm is several miles from Faberheim, our farm, but not so far that we cannot see each other on Sundays."

It was settled in minutes. They would sell their farm and move to Saskatchewan.

Chapter 19

Manitoba to Saskatchewan,1909-1910

Selling a farm is no simple matter. Especially for a widow woman, Rikka discovered.

She first approached a few of her neighbours. The women commiserated with her loss, offering tea and kind words. The men looked solemn and nodded in agreement with their wives' expressions of sympathy. None expressed any interest in buying her land.

"I know our land is not the best," Rikka confided to Marie as they mucked out the milk cows' stalls side by side. "It's hardly the worst, either. Why, just last month that bit of swamp across the road changed hands. Isn't it strange that no one makes an offer on ours? They know I am desperate to sell. And whoever heard of a farmer turning down a bargain? I think they just don't want to do business with a woman!"

Rikka, skirt hiked up and tucked into her bloomers, manhandled the loaded wheelbarrow across the packed earth floor and out the barn door to the manure pile. The old anger of a lifetime ago, when her brother had taunted her about the uselessness of girls, flared up again. *Did those men even believe women are fully adults,* she fumed?

Maybe it's not the fault of the men, or not entirely. Most mothers favour sons over daughters, just as my mother did. Just as I do, without meaning to do it. Men grow from boyhood to old age without ever questioning their privileged position. No wonder they are comfortable thinking of women as selfless creatures whose natural role is ministering to the needs of their family, or weak-minded dolls to be protected or exploited.

She looked around for her girls. There were Hjordis and Ruth, bringing in the oxen team from another day of work in the fields. Marie, her pretty face screwed up as though to prevent any of the barn-smells from reaching her nose, was removing her work-gloves and brushing bits of straw from her skirt. *Will my girls never be given the respect they have earned?*

That evening, after a supper of pan-fried potatoes and scrambled eggs, Marie helped Kris and Torolf with their homework at the kitchen table and set Thorstein to work copying his letters. Rikka brought out her mending basket and she, Hjordis and Ruth pulled their chairs in a tight circle to share the lamplight. Hjordis, as usual, tried to lighten her mother's mood.

"Don't be discouraged, Mama. Our neighbours are nice people. Someone will want to buy our farm, just wait and see."

Rikka forced a smile and nodded. "No doubt. It's just that the men are used to dealing with each other. They feel uncertain how to proceed making a business deal with a woman."

They are neighbourly and friendly enough in the ordinary run of things. Why is it so hard for them to see me as their equal?

* * *

Rikka discovered that hers was the only farm in the area currently owned by a woman. Only eight years earlier, a woman in the same circumstance might not have inherited the land. A married woman had no claim on marital property. However, in 1900, Manitoba's all-male elected legislature had passed the Married Women's Property Act, enshrining a married woman's legal right to own property and sign contracts.

Accustomed to the traditional roles of men and women, many of her neighbours found it hard to accept the validity of this new law. The existence of a husband had given Rikka, in their eyes, the right to act as his surrogate. As his widow, she fell into an indeterminate space, no longer farmwife and certainly not the legitimate owner. Rikka suspected that some of the women actively discouraged their husbands from dealing with her. A widow might safely be an object of charity; but she must not expect admittance to the domain of business.

"Best leave that to those who understand it," she was told by a young banker who drove out to the farm to offer, for a percentage, to handle things for her.

She thanked him and said she would think about it.

It was only after she and the boys spent the whole summer digging ditches to drain the water from their swampy fields and turn more of it into arable acres that one of her neighbours approached her.

"Well, Rikka, the banker tells me that you actually do have title to your land. Not like in the old country, I guess. Back there, they would have handed it over to your oldest boy, young Kris. But the banker says its okay – and the lawyer, too, he says it's fine – then I guess I should take this poor farm off your hands."

Marie spoke up pertly. "What a shame, Mr. Johnson, that you didn't make Mama that offer last winter! As it is, we have spent all those months working so hard to improve our farm – now the land is drained and will be ready for planting next spring. I really don't think we can let it go. Not now."

Her dark lashes fluttered against her ivory skin. She folded her hands demurely in her unbleached cotton dairy apron.

Rikka glared at her, aghast. Was this foolish girl determined to cost them the sale? When they were so desperate to get away?

Before she could overcome her astonishment and apologize for her daughter's rashness, Mr. Johnson cleared his throat and said, "Ah, yes, that does change things a little."

By the time their discussion concluded, he had sweetened his offer with more generous terms.

"If you can only hold off for six months or so until I have my own crop sold."

That suited Rikka to a T. After watching his buggy bounce down the lane and out of sight behind the trees, she and Marie collapsed on the doorstep and laughed till tears ran down their cheeks. The boys came running from their farmyard chores to see what was wrong.

Nothing was wrong. All went smoothly after that. They weaned the calves and sold them, as well as all the sheep, keeping back only enough livestock to see them through the winter. Three milk cows and a few dozen chickens would provide them with food and cash income from the butter, cheese, and eggs. Their last months in Teulon were spent in happy busy-ness preparing for what the youngsters thought of as a great adventure into the wilds of Saskatchewan, and Rikka hoped to be a return to comfortable old-country ways and extended family connections.

* * *

"Mama, how much longer? When will we get there?"

Thorstein stretched as tall as his sturdy frame would allow and peered out the window. After an hour of exploring the passenger car, sitting with each of his siblings in turn, and discovering the conductor did indeed live on board the train, his excitement over the train ride had abated. The country he watched speed past the window looked to his eyes much like the hummocky fields and bluffs of trees he had seen all his life. Sitting still in a confined space was hard for a small boy used to running off excess energy outside. Rikka could see he was getting restless.

"We have many miles to go yet, my dear." She glanced at Torolf and Kris, several seats ahead of them, their heads barely visible as they bent over the checkerboard on the seat between them. Her three daughters across the aisle from them shared two facing seats with a young woman who seemed to be travelling alone. "Why don't you go and sit with Torolf and Kris for a while. And tell Marie I want her to come to me."

Marie dropped into the seat beside her. "Do you know, Mama, I think we are the only people in this car who have been in Canada for more than a few weeks? Everyone I've talked to is fresh off the boat. It makes me feel like an old-timer. You see that girl sitting beside Ruth? Well, she came all by herself from a little town in Scotland to join her brother. He made the crossing a few years ago and now he has a general store in that town with the funny name — what is it again? Oh yes, Moose Jaw!"

"I am glad you girls are making friends with her," Rikka said. "She must be lonely coming all this way by herself."

"Oh, she says it has been a great adventure," Marie declared, sounding almost envious of the girl's freedom. "But she is surprised to see snowbanks this late in the year. You should have seen her face when I told her we often have another snowstorm, even this late in May, before winter is really over."

Rikka's mind was too full of her own family's concerns to spare more than cursory attention to a stranger's shock at the tricks this land might play on them.

"Marie, I have an idea for you to consider. If this farmer we are going to work for is a decent sort of fellow, as Kristine says he is, we might keep a few cows of our own. You and Hjordis could ..."

"No, Mama, do not even think of it." Marie turned away from Rikka, head high and her lips pressed together. "Do you know what they called us in Teulon? Do you think I want to be known all my life as the Norske dairymaid?"

"But - but - I thought you enjoyed the trips to town, making bargains with the storekeeper and meeting other people. You and Hjordis have such skill ..."

"Hjordis likes it, Mama. She has a real gift for getting the butter just so and she has patience for that whole tedious process of cheesemaking. I hated it. I only did it all those years because you expected it of me. And you needed my help. But it is high time you realize I am a grown-up woman, not your little girl to be ordered about. I have my own plans. My plans do not include wasting my life on a farm making cheese. Or shoveling cow dirt."

Rikka stared at her for a moment, then said stiffly, "And what, may I ask, are these plans of yours? To leave your family? Abandon me and your little brothers and sisters?"

"Mama, how can you think that? Of course, I will help you and the youngsters get settled in this new place. But – but – don't you see it is time for me to think of my own future, too?"

Marie's face crumpled.

"You must let me choose how I help. I can find my own work, as a saleslady in a clothing store or trimming hats for a milliner. I could do as Father did, find work that suits my talents and send you money to help out. I am sure that is what Father would want me to do, if he were alive."

Rikka's anger died, quenched by the tears in her daughter's eyes. She spoke placatingly.

"Yes, Marie, you are right. I forget that you are the age I was when your father and I married. Just promise me to stay with us a little longer. There may be some work suitable for you in this new place."

A memory of her own brief taste of independence, when she taught music at the folkskule, made her catch her breath. She saw clearly for the first time how far out of reach that type of employment would be for Marie, an immigrant child whose formal education had been cut short by the demands of the homestead.

She squeezed Marie's hands and said, "I will not stand in your way. Just promise me that you will not leave me to go to Chicago."

Marie hugged her and smiled a sad little smile. She would make no such promise.

Rikka realized this rail journey presented her with an opportunity to discover her children's secret dreams – dreams that she must either squash or support. Living as they had, united under the pressure of acquiring the bare necessities - food, clothing, shelter - she had forgotten to see them as individuals. Marie's words had shaken her. What other surprises might her brood be prepared to spring on her?

Over the next hours, Rikka learned much about her children. Hjordis confirmed Marie's assessment of her ability and said she would prefer having Ruth help her in her dairy work, as Ruth, unlike Marie, did not mind getting her hands dirty. She had always liked working outside with the livestock.

"Mama, I don't like your idea of trying to keep a few cows on another person's farm. We have been doing everything by ourselves for years now, without a man to help us. Why shouldn't we do it again, with better land, a place we choose ourselves? We should get our own farm, not too far from Aunty Kristine and Uncle Odin's place. Don't you remember, Aunty wrote that there might still be some land available for homesteading? Close to a river with good water? Where it never floods like it does at Teulon?"

Rikka agreed that might be a possibility. "But it will be several years before the boys are old enough to file on a homestead – they have to be at least eighteen."

"Mama, I found something you should see. I clipped it out of that newspaper Mrs. Johnson had wrapped around the buns she brought us. Here, let me show you."

Hjordis rummaged in her bag and brought out the clipping. "Synopsis of Canadian Northwest Land Regulations," she read. Slowly she continued, glancing up at her mother to be certain she was paying attention to every word. "Any person who is the sole head of a family or any male over eighteen years of age may homestead a quarter-section of available Dominion land in Manitoba, Saskatchewan or Alberta."

"Any person who is the sole head of a family," she repeated. "That's you, Mama, the sole head of our family. You don't have to wait until Kris is grown up!"

Rikka took the clipping and studied it. Yes, this might change everything. Aloud she said, "That is something I should investigate, Hjordis. But we don't want to jump from the frying pan into the fire. We just escaped from one homestead. I want to know something about the land before I take on another farm. Working as a housekeeper will give me the opportunity to see how people do things, meet other farm families, get to know the land."

Hjordis looked pleased that her mother was willing to consider her suggestion.

"And Mama, Marie and I agree that we should both find work elsewhere while you work as a housekeeper. Helping on our own farm is one thing. It is quite a different thing to work on a farm belonging to someone else. I want to be paid for my work, not do chores for my room and board."

Rikka pursed her lips and nodded in agreement. She felt ashamed that she had been able to give her girls so little in exchange for the years they had sacrificed toiling on the farm at Teulon.

Hjordis continued. "I wrote to Aunty Kristine during the winter and asked her to help me find something. She says we will be arriving at the perfect time for me to find paid employment. With all the spring's work, calving and lambing and planting, there will be lots of families looking for a girl like me."

Indeed! No doubt there will many a young bachelor, too, looking for a pretty girl to cook his meals and warm his bed as well as help on the farm, Rikka thought.

She merely said, "You have a good head on your shoulders, Hjordis. We will see what comes of this."

Next was Ruth. Rikka realized while she had been so occupied over the past months, first dealing with the legalities of getting title to their property after Mentz's death, then disposing of their land and making arrangements for their new life, her children had been making their own plans. Ruth echoed Hjordis.

"We should get our own farm, Mama."

Ruth said if Hjordis wanted to work some place else, that was fine with her. She, Ruth, the youngest daughter, squared her sturdy shoulders and said to Rikka, "I am quite able to look after livestock myself. I can take care of the cattle, and sheep, and chickens, too. The boys will help. If we get a horse and wagon, the boys can make deliveries in town of milk and cream and eggs."

Rikka asked her, "What else do you think you might want to do? Is there any work that you would especially like to learn?"

"I want to learn to make things," she said. "I don't mean just spinning, knitting, sewing, baking. I already know how to do all that. I want to make things that people cannot make for themselves and might buy. What do you think, Mama? What could I make?"

Rikka considered carefully, thinking that Ruth had already acquired an impressive list of useful skills. "Let's wait until we get settled and then talk about this again, Ruth. Maybe you could bake bread and cakes to sell to bachelor farmers. Or knit sweaters?"

Ruth was doubtful but returned to her seat and told Kris it was his turn to go talk to Mama. By this time Rikka felt drained. She was tempted to dispense with the intensity of a private interview and have Kris and Torolf come together. They were almost always together anyway, and she doubted either one had a thought the other one could not finish for him.

In the end, she was glad she had not deprived herself or them of this rare opportunity for an uninterrupted one-to-one conversation. The two boys only agreed on one thing, that it would be "really keen" to deliver eggs and cream to town together, just the two of them, without any of their sisters riding herd on them. Rikka explained patiently that might be a good plan for some time in the future, not right away. When she asked each what work they imagined doing when they were grownup, their answers could not have been more different.

Kris said, "I want to build things. Houses and big buildings in the city, like Dad was working on in Chicago."

Rikka smiled at him. "It sounds as though you will be in the right place for that. Since the railway reached their town last year, Kristine says that houses and businesses are springing up almost over night."

Rikka made a mental note to ask Kristine and Odin about carpenters in the area. Kris was already old enough to apprentice with a builder and learn his trade.

Torolf, however, touched her heart. His dream was to learn to play the piano. "Papa used to say that you played the piano all the time in Norway. And you played so well, even the Queen came to hear you. I want to play like that."

Rikka's days as a pianist now seemed in the distant past, but she decided that must change. Someone, Kristine or one of the cousins, or the new church Kristine had written about, would have a piano. She promised Torolf she would teach him to play.

Torolf's only other request was, when they had their own farm again, that they get as many different animals as possible. Sheep, goats, ducks, geese, cattle, horses, chickens – he loved them all.

Thorstein returned to her side and snuggled onto her lap. The train whistle blew as they stopped at one small town after another. Passengers gathered up belongings and disembarked, others clambered aboard with satchels and suitcases. Long stretches of open prairie lay golden gray in the setting sun. Lingering traces of snow had disappeared. The steam locomotive roared and puffed. The clickety clack of the wheels accompanied the rhythmic swaying of the coach. The last light faded from the sky. They pulled their coats around themselves and slept.

Chapter 20

Saskatchewan, Easter Sunday, 1913

Rikka's fingers caressed the keys as the last notes of the recessional faded. She removed the hymnal from the piano and lowered the keyboard, then turned to smile at the woman who now stood beside her. She had immediately sensed Kristine's presence. In all the bustle and noise of people rising from pews, chatting with their neighbours, and retrieving coats shed during the service, she recognized her sister's footstep.

It felt like old times. The comfortable network of family friendships had slipped over and around her like a warm shawl almost from the first moment she and her children had clambered onto the platform at Elbow's CPR Station. Odin and Kristine were there to welcome her, along with a smiling crowd of local people who seemed to make it a daily ritual to meet the six p.m. northbound train and greet newcomers.

Now, almost four years later, her spirit was calm, her mind at peace. Once more she belonged to a community where she and her gift of music filled a place. The assurance of familiar faces, kindly voices and mutual understanding had restored her confidence.

She discovered how much she needed that confidence during her first months in Saskatchewan. More adjustments than she expected had awaited her.

* * *

Is it because I am getting old? She felt ashamed that what to others might seem like minor changes felt to her like major alterations. Why should a woman who had lost four children in tragic circumstances be so disturbed by the normal progression of children leaving home? *Maybe,* she thought, *that is the root of the problem … we no longer have a home!* A few weeks after arriving in Saskatchewan, Marie announced that she had, with the help of her acquaintance on the train, been hired as sales lady by a posh clothing store in Moose Jaw. Hjordis accepted the offer of work on a farm owned by neighbours of Odin and Kristine. As hired girl, she helped with barnyard chores and garden as well as the unending labour of a household with young children. Kris, eager to take on his responsibilities as the eldest son, signed on as apprentice with a building contractor in the village of Elbow. Meanwhile, Rikka and Ruth and the two younger boys had settled precariously into the home of a widower who seemed to expect his housekeeper and her children to intuitively fill every role his struggling farm required.

I have managed a household for thirty years and run my own farm without help for the past five, she fumed inwardly. *Taking orders like a servant is not for me.*

She had kept the newspaper clipping Hjordis showed her on the train. Careful inquiries made through Odin and her nephews ensured that she and Hjorids had indeed understood the wording correctly. She, Rikka, a widow woman now almost fifty years old, was legally able to apply for a homestead in the Canadian prairie on the same terms as any eighteen-year-old male.

It took no prodding from her children nor helpful suggestions from Odin for her to avail herself of the first opportunity to plan a visit to the land office in Moose Jaw. Rikka knew the land she wanted. She had circled the quarter section on the rural municipal map. She had made discreet inquiries. It was not yet claimed. When she had first glimpsed that broad valley from the train, she felt drawn to it. The location was ideal, not far from the village and just a few miles beyond the Aiktow railway siding. She remembered it was near a small creek that fed into the South Saskatchewan River. One afternoon in July, telling the farmer who employed her that she needed canning supplies from the general store in Elbow, she borrowed his horse and buggy.

"Ruth, you must look after supper for me tonight. I might not be back in time for chores, either."

Ruth frowned and then winked at her mother as she guessed her real errand.

At the last minute, Rikka called Torolf and Thorstein to come with her. *The boys should see it. If I do get the land, some day it will be their farm.*

After making her purchases in town and giving the boys a penny each to buy hard candy, she turned the horse's head away from the trail they had followed into town, away from land sprawling flat and treeless to the horizon. They detoured onto a prairie trail heading out the western edge of the village, skirting the deep broad valley of the South Saskatchewan River with its groves of elm, aspen and cottonwood. They descended into a shallow valley dotted with gray clumps of wolf willow and thorny buffalo berry bushes. Wild roses bloomed beside the trail and scarlet tiger lilies popped up through the grass. Rikka was more interested in the lush green grass itself – *good pasture* – and saskatoon bushes hanging with purple fruit – *winter preserves for the picking.* Torolf and Thorstein shouted with delight at long-legged jackrabbits bounding out of the shrubs, almost causing their horse to bolt, then sat in silent awe when a spotted fawn stood curiously watching them pass. Rikka felt a peace and stillness she had not know since leaving Norway.

A week later, on her day off, she arrived at the railway station early in the morning to board the southbound train. Her map, the description of the land location - NW quarter of section 34, township 24, range 5 West of the 3rd Meridian - and papers confirming her as a widow and legal head of her family were safely tucked in her reticule. She arrived at the Land Office ahead of anyone else other than a tall shaggy young man who looked to her as though he had spent the night waiting at the door. He turned, stared hard at her, nodded in acknowledgement of her "Good morning," then looked away. She studied his back, trying hard not to notice the smell of unwashed clothes and sweating feet. She was glad he did not try to strike up a conversation with her.

"Well, you are the first woman to file on land in Saskatchewan this week," said the young agent. "In fact, you are the very first woman I have ever helped file homestead papers."

He gave a snort of laughter and pointed to the tall man who was leaving the building. "I guess it's a day of firsts. Not seen anyone like him before today, either. That Finn must be tough as nails. Says he walked all the way from Minnesota to file on land his brother told him about. And will walk all the way back to get his wife and kids after he proves up his homestead."

Rikka looked out the window at the man's retreating back. *No wonder his shoes stank, and his clothes were dirty! Poor fellow. Will he ever see his family again?*

She wished she had spoken to him.

* * *

Glad as she was to leave the position of housekeeper, she graciously thanked the widower for giving her employment in her first season in Saskatchewan and pretended to not understand his meaning when he clumsily suggested she might stay on as his wife if she did not care to be his housekeeper. *Thank the good Lord, I have other resources!* She had been able to save most of the money from the sale of the farm at Teulon and now found good use for it.

Throughout the fine days of autumn, the valley hills echoed with hammering as the young builder whom Kris served as apprentice directed his eager crew. Ruth proved to have a good eye for measurements; Kris understood the over-all plan and ensured no mistakes were made; Torolf caught on quickly to any skill required of him, and six-year-old Thorstein enthusiastically embraced his new role as "go-fer."

Something wonderful happened as they built. The land seemed to embrace them, to welcome them. It felt to the boys as though the little house in the valley had always been home. They were once more part of a community - not the deep-rooted community Rikka had known in Norway but a new one where everyone was a transplant struggling to get rooted. All were buffeted by the same storms, all suffered the same shortages of tea and sugar, all joined forces to build schools and churches. Rikka felt that her children had arrived at the beginning, or close to the beginning, and could make this their own place.

The village of Elbow was only months old when they arrived. Like most prairie towns, its location was pre-ordained by the railroad. All the villages were laid out the same way, a grid of streets oriented to the rail line. To a casual passerby they looked remarkably similar, with their false-fronted businesses on main street and their train station the centre of activity. But that was just the skeleton, the framework; those who knew the heart and soul of the place could plainly see the differences. Every little hamlet, every cluster of farms, had a distinct personality reflecting the combined natures of its citizens. One community might make a name for itself by its baseball team, another be famous for its St. Patrick's Day dance. Celebrations or ceremonies performed for the first time in short order became customs, then traditions and then unbreakable laws.

This was doubly true of the Norwegian Lutheran communities, bound together by ties of blood, belief and language. Odin and Kristine and their family were among the founding members of Skudesnes, the country church northeast of the village of Loreburn. Odin had developed his natural and spiritual gifts and served as Bible teacher, sometimes as lay pastor. Eight miles down the line in the village of Elbow, another Norwegian Lutheran congregation welcomed Rikka and her family. They built their white-steepled church in the village, named it Bethel, and asked Rikka to be organist. From the first Sunday service, her position was secure. People long starved for choral music and congregational singing congratulated themselves that their church home was now complete.

Rikka would never forget that first congregational meeting in the new church building. Her savings were depleted. She had poured everything she had into her house, a lean-to barn, and enough stock to get them established. There was no money left over. Rikka knew at this meeting the council would announce the subscriptions, amounts owed by each family for church expenses. Every adult was expected to contribute a set amount, as well as make gift offerings. Rikka hoped she had set aside enough, having denied the boys new boots and given Ruth her own winter coat.

Her heart sank as she listened to the church elder read aloud the amounts required. *It's too much. It will be another year before I can pay my share!*

Then she heard her own name read, and looked up, startled. "However, it has been unanimously agreed that Rikka be exempt from this subscription, in recognition of her valuable service as organist."

Tears flowed down her cheeks as she glanced at her neighbours, who were nodding their agreement with the decision.

* * *

The two Norwegian Lutheran congregations shared a pastor and alternated services on special occasions so families and friends could celebrate Christmas, Thanksgiving, and Easter together. This Easter it was Bethel's turn. Rikka's little house in the valley would be filled to bursting.

Most of the worshipers gathered outside after the service to greet friends and neighbours. Purified inside and out by Saturday night bath and Sunday morning worship, they relished this time of leisure after church and before dinner. The church bell tolled its joyous message, Christ is risen. Rikka and Kristine gathered up their heavy cloaks and walked down the aisle to the vestibule side by side, comfortable as only sisters and old friends can be. Brilliant early spring sunshine splashed through the tall windows lining both sides of the church and fell across the two, accenting their identical jawlines and long narrow noses. Any stranger seeing them for the first time would know them to be sisters. Although stooped, Kristine was still the taller while Rikka was the broader and stronger of the two. Kristine, the elder by several years, was not much greyer than Rikka. Both wore their thick braids coiled like crowns under their Sunday hats. Their dresses were long and dark and while not exactly dowdy, had been designed for comfort and long wear rather than beauty. They presented a flawless depiction of mature female respectability.

They paused in the vestibule to exchange the traditional Easter greeting with Pastor Hagen. *Sandelig han er oppstanden!* It was a source of deep satisfaction to Rikka, as to all the older parishioners, that their Pastor conducted the entire worship service, from hymn singing through sermon, in Norwegian. They may have to struggle with English in everyday matters of business, buying and selling and dealing with government officials, but in areas that really mattered - that is, in spiritual and family matters - only the old familiar tongue was used. How else could you pray and expect to be heard? The young folks might grumble all they liked, Norwegian would remain the language of church and home for this generation.

They stepped out into the crisp still-wintry air. Both women instinctively looked around to locate their children, although "children" was a term they rarely used for their grown or almost grown brood. Rikka saw Hjordis deep in conversation with her beau, Ingvald, whose farm adjoined the one where Hjordis worked. They would marry before the year was out, Rikka thought.

We must find a moment this afternoon to show Hjordis the tablecloths and pillowcases Ruth and I have finished for her hope chest.

Kris and Torolf stood with a group of young men clustered around Otto, their twenty-year-old cousin. Of all Kristine and Odin's dozen children, only Aadel, a daughter who intended to remain single and run her own farm, and sons Otto and Arne still lived with their parents. The cousins had grown close in the few years they had been reunited in this prairie community. They thought nothing of riding horseback eight or ten miles to share a ballgame or an afternoon of music. Rikka smiled at them, thinking how splendid it would be at her house today to hear their strong young voices blending and harmonizing.

Kristine hurried over to a sleigh where her grandchildren, Gudrun's and Julius' three little ones, waved and called to her. Rikka had invited them as well as the rest of the family for Easter dinner, but Gudrun had told her before church this morning that little Mildred had a cold and earache. They would return home immediately after church.

Marius and Signe, newlyweds and still childless, greeted Rikka with smiles and hugs. Signe was more reserved towards her aunt than her brothers were, but even so, Rikka felt a special affection for her. That may have had something to do with her choice of husband. Rikka had liked Marius from the first time the youngster had come to her for music lessons at Karstenoya. Resuming her old friendship with him, his parents and siblings had been one of the attractions of this community. Marius and Signe would join them for an afternoon of music, after they had dinner with Marius' parents, Anna and Andreas, and after Rikka's own dinner guests had been amply fed.

Ruth, always high spirited and ready for fun, dashed past red-cheeked and laughing, snowball in hand, and flung it at Arne. Other young folk joined in the game. They disappeared around the corner of the church as a few of the grownups smiled and others frowned disapprovingly. Rikka hurried after them and called, "Ruth, come here. We are ready to go home."

When oh when will you learn to stop drawing attention to yourself. Almost sixteen and you still forget to behave like a woman.

Even with the supposed freedom afforded by this new land, Rikka knew well enough that a woman, especially a young and pretty one, must be circumspect or risk losing everything. For a woman, her reputation was, indeed, everything. A female schoolteacher could be fired for entertaining a male visitor in her home. A widow with unmarried daughters was in a particularly delicate position if there were no male relatives to provide a shield of respectability. Rikka wondered if Kristine and Odin knew how much comfort their unimpeachable name provided. It was through them, she believed, she had been first offered the position as organist, through them that Hjordis had obtained work with a kindly family.

If only Marie had followed her example, instead of going off alone to work in the city.

Rikka remembered the boys singing a ditty composed by one of the young wags in town that caused much merriment.

This town is good to live in
And as sporty as can be.
The Ladies Aid, they run it.
And that suits me!

It needed no translation for her to get the import of the message. Sport was for men only.

Ruth in tow, Rikka waited for Kris to bring the sleigh around. Torolf, Thorstein, Ruth and their cousin Arne piled into the back as Kris helped his mother settle her skirts on the seat beside him. The runners whispered and hissed as they slid smoothly onto the icy main street. They passed through the business part of town, boisterously optimistic in its newness and size. Only four years old, the town already boasted general stores, draymen, blacksmith shop, Chinese laundry and restaurants, besides the big hotel and livery stable facing the train station. Today everything was shuttered. Sunday quiet lay over the usually bustling village.

The return of cold weather had firmed up the snow cover on the trail that led south and down the valley. The route, they had

262

been told, was part of the old wagon trail used by traders and native prairie dwellers of the last century. North from the elbow of the South Saskatchewan River it led eventually to the small city of Saskatoon; heading south, it carried on to the frontier town of Swift Current. This three-mile segment of the trail their sleigh travelled in winter, their buggy in summer, south over the river hills and down the broad valley. Little homesteads had sprung up on almost every quarter section. Thorstein recited the names of their neighbours as they passed. These were their friends, even those who spoke different languages and attended different churches, all having arrived within a few years of each other. They relied on one another for barn raisings and ballgames, for help in blizzard or sickness, for celebrations of weddings or birthdays. Rikka no longer felt like a newcomer alone in a strange land. In this place, at this time, in the beginning of it all, they were equals. Intentional or not, they were building a community in their own image. No one knew what it might become.

The sleigh clattered over the little creek and stopped at the door of the house for Rikka and Ruth to get out before Kris drove on past the barn to turn the horses out in the corral. Rikka paused for a moment as she always did to enjoy the view. She felt again how expansive this land was, all far horizons and big sky. To the west, the valley opened onto the broad river valley with high hills on the far side marking the skyline. Up the south slope of the valley lay unbroken prairie where the boys had found bison bones scattered in the grass. To the north, Aiktow Creek provided water for the lower pasture and sometimes, if an ice jam caused the river to flood into the creek, yielded fish. Even in the terrible prairie fires of last summer, they were safe in the valley. It seemed a world apart.

Rikka hurried inside to prepare for their guests. The young men took over stabling the horses while Odin followed Kristine inside. *Even without Gudrun's family we will be ten at the table.* The goose she had roasted would serve twice that many, even with the hollow legs of half a dozen young men to fill. The potatoes were ready to put on the stove and would be cooked by the time various small tables were fitted together and covered with her long white linen cloth to make one banquet table. Pies, cookies, bread, butter, fresh cream for the coffee, all was ready.

And while Odin dozes in the rocking chair and the young men stretch their legs outside and the girls clean up the dishes, Kristine and I will have a cup of coffee. I will tell her, but only her, why Marie had to leave for Chicago so suddenly. And why we are not likely to see her again.

Then Marius and Signe will arrive. And the boys will come back inside, teasing the girls for taking so long with the dishes. Odin will call for music. I will play my piano. Marius will play his violin. The others will join in, singing.

We will forget all that troubles us.

Chapter 21

Saskatchewan,1914-1918

News of the assassination of the Archduke in Sarajevo reached Saskatchewan almost as quickly as it did the rest of the world, that summer of 1914. Rikka read the headline in the weekly Farmer's Advocate and Home Journal and wondered what all the fuss was about. Those Balkan countries were always in some sort of turmoil, it seemed to her. She scarcely gave the incident another thought. *Nothing a decent Norwegian-Canadian mother need concern herself about.*

But that was four years ago.

It turned out to be an event to concern all mothers. Still regarded as a colony of the British Empire by the motherland, Canada was naturally expected to send her sons to fight and die in the trenches and battle fields of Europe. By 1918, this country of only eight million people had given over half a million of her children to the conflict. More than a third of those became casualties, dying in the mud of Flanders or sent home

266

wounded and maimed. No corner of the world escaped the Great War. Even neutral Norway was drawn in as an ally of England.

When Rikka realized that under Canada's Military Service Act of 1917 two of her three sons would be drafted, she walked the windswept hills for hours weeping. Her boys never saw the tears. She returned to the house with squared shoulders and set mouth and her voice under firm control.

"At least you will be fighting on the right side," she said to Torolf and Kris that evening.

"How will you manage the farm without us, Mama?"

Kris shifted his broad shoulders, conscious of the burden he bore as the eldest son. His sisters had left home, all more or less happily living their own independent lives. Hjordis had married her industrious Ingvald and was absorbed by babies and the many duties of a farmwife. Marie never returned from the States but wrote to tell of her marriage. She now had another child as well as the baby girl born before she left Canada. As for Ruth – well, her marriage surprised no one except possibly Walter, who, stoic Scot that he was, never quite got over the shock of being the one chosen by Ruth from all her suitors. They had a child, a farm, and Rikka no longer worried about what Ruth might do next.

With all her daughters grown up and gone, and Kris and Torolf called up to do their duty for king and country, only she and Thorstein would be left on the farm.

"Don't you worry about us."

Rikka brushed a lock of brown hair from Kris's forehead as though brushing away all trivial concerns. "I'll get one of the neighbours to plant that oat field for us, in exchange for part of the crop. We can do the haying and look after the livestock ourselves. Thorstein will continue to deliver eggs and cream to our customers in town, and instead of making butter to sell I will ship the extra cream. With our big garden – well, we will manage."

She poured them each another cup of coffee and stirred a generous dollop of cream into hers.

"Only promise me to take care of each other. Those awful stories we have heard about the trenches, the sickness, the rats, the poisonous gas – they are all true. You've read Otto's letters from the front."

She took another sip of her coffee, struggling to keep down the frantic thoughts that threatened to strangle her.

"And you know some of those young men, boys you knew, won't ever come home."

Torolf nodded. "We know it's bad, Mama. But we are young and strong. None stronger!" He flexed his biceps and grinned with uncharacteristic bravado.

Kris studied her face, his kind blue eyes crinkled in a frown. "Don't worry about us, we will watch out for each other. But I wonder how you and Thorstein will get on by yourselves, Mama. You must write to us every week."

Rikka, always earnest, spoke with even more intensity. "Of course, we will write often! But you have no need to be concerned. When you boys think of home, you must never waste a moment worrying about us. Think only how proud we are, how proud we will always be of you. Bravely doing your duty for your country."

She almost choked on the last words. It was not in her tradition or her nature to glorify war, especially a war that seemed so vilely unnecessary. She could knit socks and hope to keep their feet warm, but what about their hearts and minds? Would they come home hardened or broken, disillusioned or bitter? *I can love my children, give my life for them, but in the end, I cannot protect them.*

An illusion of confidence she would give them, along with her prayers. She could not let her boys go with doubts or fears. Putting aside her own feelings, as she had so many times in the past, she was determined to give at least token support to a cause that might take the lives of her sons.

* * *

As it turned out, no such sacrifice was required. They reported for duty in Regina in May,1918. Either because the war was nearing its end, or because the recruiting officer had learned the sad history of a pioneer widow already bereft of four children, or because the army really needed musicians, both Torolf and Kris were assigned to the military band.

In November 1918, their battalion had not yet been sent overseas when the armistice was signed. Rikka's fears switched from hellish battlefields to overcrowded barracks as the terrible flu that was secretly ravaging the troops followed soldiers returning from the front. Long suppressed memories surfaced: the shipboard contagions that trapped her family in Quebec, the hidden diseases that stole Aksel and Asbjorne and Gunhild from her, the stealthy bacterium that weakened Mentz's bones. Might this new illness that people called the Spanish Flu take more of her family?

This time it seemed heaven heard her prayers. The flu skipped over their barracks and no accidents befell them. On January 27, 1919, both young men were discharged

270

from the army and returned home to much rejoicing and with new dreams and goals. They had changed and so had the land.

Many of the businesses previously lining the main street of the village had closed or changed hands. Others had opened to take their places. Some had expanded and grown during the war. A few individuals had even become wealthy. With the war over and a new prosperity promised, optimism reigned. All arable land had been claimed by homesteaders. Farms dotted every mile of the wagon trails that still passed for country roads. The prairie sod released the stored nutrients of ten thousand years and produced bumper crops. Elegant two-story houses replaced the sod shacks or shanties on some farms. Big hip-roofed barns appeared on others.

To Torolf and Kris, little seemed to have changed on their mother's farm. More silver glinted in Rikka's brown braid, but her bearing was erect as ever. Thorstein had added inches and muscle but still had the same boyish grin. It took a few weeks for them to see how much he had matured in their absence.

Rikka was more aware of the changes that had taken place in Kris and Torolf. She surveyed them with stern pleasure, seeing in little mannerisms how like Torolf was to her own long-dead brother, and noticing how much Kris resembled Mentz. Over the next months she realized the likenesses were not entirely superficial. She was reminded once again that she could not expect her children to follow any path but their own. They were molded to fit a world she found increasingly difficult to understand.

It was a fine evening in late spring. A meadowlark's rich trilling song cascaded through the valley. After supper, Torolf suggested they all take their coffee out to the kaffe stua, as they called the sheltered area beneath a solitary elm tree not far from the house. From spring through summer until the last warm day of October, this was the spot where they welcomed family and friends with coffee and cookies, or where one or the other of them seized rare moments of leisure in their busy days. Rikka kept a few old chairs set out and Thorstein had built a bench and table beneath the tree's overhanging branches. Here they were sheltered by groves of aspen to the north and south, yet still had a fine view of the setting sun across the river hills. A light breeze wafted the sweet scent of wolf willow from the sandhills.

"Mama, I want to take over the farm," Torolf began. He spoke as he always did, with a firm voice and a manner that seldom acknowledged another point of view was possible, let alone worth considering. "You have enough to do with your chickens and geese and ducks, your big garden, your spinning and your music. We - that is, Kris and Thorstein and I - want to lighten your load. I want you to put me in charge of the crops and the livestock. I have some ideas about expanding the farm. I've been reading about different breeds and ..."

Rikka interrupted him. "But Torolf, you know our custom – it is Kris, as the eldest son, who has first right to take over the farm."

Now it was Kris's turn to interrupt. "Mama, Torolf and I have already discussed this. We will work together for the next few years while we help Thorstein get started in a career."

Rikka turned to her youngest son and smiled a rueful smile. "You have been a great help to me, Thorstein, but I know your heart is not in the farm. You want to be a builder and a businessman, don't you? Like your father."

Thorstein laughed and nodded. "We have another surprise for you, Mama. Tell her, Kris!"

Kris produced a letter from his jacket pocket. "Do you remember, Mama, when Father died, the builder he worked for wrote to you? Well, Marie kept that letter and she got in touch with him when she went to Chicago. He helped her find work. She wrote to us when we were called up and told us he had asked her about us. She said that when we were discharged from our army service, we should get in touch with him. So we did."

"I wrote to him that Torolf and I want to help this kid brother of ours get started in a career in architecture, since he is the only one of us who was smart enough to attend school regularly."

Thorstein groaned, and Kris gave him a friendly jab in the ribs. "Not your fault, little brother, that Torolf and I had a farm to run while you were still in primary school."

"So anyway, Marianne sent us a packet from the University of Illinois, and Thorstein has applied to the school of architecture. If he completes his course, there will be a job waiting for him in Chicago."

Kris handed her the letter. Rikka took it and smoothed the paper as she read, then handed it back to Kris, but her eyes were on Thorstein.

"You will leave here. To live in the States." Rikka spoke slowly as though struggling to comprehend what this would mean.

"Yes, Mama. Not right away, of course. We will help on the farm for the rest of this year. And I will try to find extra work to help pay my travel expenses."

Kris waved his arm, taking in the farmyard and surrounding valley. "We love what you have done for us here, Mama. But you know, Torolf is the one who understands it best. He is a farmer at heart. Thorstein is not. I'm not sure that I am, either, but I am going to give it a shot. Meanwhile, this is an opportunity for our little brother to get a foot in the door of the building business. Maybe I will join him eventually. Chicago is booming. It would be exciting to be part of that."

That summer Rikka had to remind herself often that she should be glad for them, glad that they made plans for their future, knew what they wanted and knew how to get it. Thorstein might in a few years be established in his career. She knew that this farm would never have supported them all, it was barely enough for her alone. Torolf and Kris could apply for the Soldier Settlement Loan to buy more land, equipment and livestock, whatever they needed to make the farm profitable. For the time being at least, she would give up worrying. *Sufficient unto the day are the troubles thereof.*

With their futures in some fashion settled, each member of the little household seemed determined to make the most of their last summer together in the valley. Every sunny afternoon was reason enough for a picnic and every fine evening an occasion for music. Hardly a day went by without a wagonload or buggy-full of cousins careening down the trail over the creek to the little homestead. Excursions to the river for berry picking or fishing, family picnics and coffee parties brought friends from miles around. As one of them described it in later years, "We sang all the way there and all the way home again."

Maybe the losses they had suffered made them more grateful for the losses they had been spared. So many loved ones were gone. Rikka had experienced the sharp grief of separation once again when her sister Kristine died in 1915. Even with Kristine gone, the bonds they had forged between the two families held firm and became ever more precious because of their transience. The cousins treasured their closeness.

When her brother-in-law Odin drove into her yard on a summer morning waving a letter and shouting, "Rikka! Rikka! My boy Otto is coming home!" her joy was almost as great as his. Otto home from overseas, all their boys together again! There was no question that a special celebration must be planned. And where else would the family choose to gather but right here? Within the sheltering hills that rimmed the valley, Rikka's homestead was the obvious place for summer gatherings. War over, peace signed, troops decommissioned! Fields planted, gardens growing, days long and sunny! It was July, 1919, and the last of their boys was coming home. What a glorious time!

The day before Otto was due to arrive, Torolf, Kris, and Thorstein, together with an assortment of cousins, laboured until sunset putting up heavy canvas tents and dragging tables and chairs to the kaffe stua. By midmorning of the big day, wagons and buggies were arriving at the makeshift campground. Youngsters raced here and there in a frenzy of excitement. All the older children helped carry food boxes and baskets piled high with fried chicken, potato salad, saskatoon pie, angel-food cakes, coffee cakes and dinner buns, cookies and doughnuts. Almost every young woman carried a baby on her hip. Hjordis and Ingvald, Ruth and Walter, Marius and Signe, Gudrun and Julius, each brought something special. Marius had his violin. When Kris saw Odin carrying a case holding Otto's long idle cornet, he disappeared into the house and emerged with his own basso to set beside it. The delicious smell of bubbling coffee rose from lard pails suspended over the campfire.

"Grampa, Grampa, see what I found!"

Odin presided over the festivities from a comfortably shaded chair, a benevolent patriarch, as pleased by the spotted toad brought him by his six-year-old grandson as the bouquet of tiger lilies Hjordis set beside him. Rikka stood by the big plank table with a smile creasing her face.

Ragna's husband Ole drove slowly over the rutted trail into the yard, careful of his new Chevrolet. As the owner of the only motor vehicle in the family, he had been awarded the honour of meeting Otto's train in Elbow and bringing him to the festivity.

"No, no," he said to Rikka as his passengers spilled out, "I can't stop now. I must get back into town. I will just wait at the station for Otto."

He finally yielded to Rikka's hospitality and stayed long enough for a cup of coffee and a slice of his favourite pie before put-putting back over the creek and along the trail north to Elbow.

Rikka did not know whether she wanted to smile or scold when, shortly after Ole left, whoops of laughter and the clatter of buggy wheels turned all heads to the south. There came Kris, Thorstein and Torolf with a blond giant standing between them waving his cap! Otto was home!

The three brothers had plotted a surprise of their own. Without anyone noticing, they'd slipped away to meet Otto's train at the Aiktow siding, south of the valley. They knew it always stopped there briefly.

"If we missed it, we knew you would be in Elbow," Kris explained later to a disgruntled Ole. "As it was, we got Otto here half an hour early. No harm done, right, Ole?"

Ole scowled. He was none too pleased when, after waiting in vain for his brother-in-law to get off the train in Elbow, he had returned to discover the joke that had been played on him. Ragna brought him his coffee and another piece of pie. Good strong coffee and apple pie have a wonderful way of healing wounded pride. After enjoying a fat cigar, he smiled again.

The youngsters who had already slipped away for a swim in the river hung their swimsuits to dry from the big elm's branches and the old folks set their chairs in its shade. The table was spread with white cloths and loaded with the best things to eat. The family was together.

A breeze rustled through the leaves of the kaffe stua tree. Ruth came up behind Rikka and slipped an arm around her.

"Mama, don't you feel it? The spirits of our dear ones, all around us?"

Ruth had an unsettling way of referring to the dead as though they had just left the room and might pop back in at any moment. It usually made Rikka uncomfortable to hear Ruth talking this way, but this time she leaned against Ruth's strong young shoulder, closed her eyes, and listened to the rustle of the leaves. *So many memories*. She could almost see Kristine smiling. She thought how happy Mentz would have been to see them all here. *Who knows but that he, Kristine and*

Ingeborg, Aksel, Asbjorne - and yes, even little Gunhild - might somehow be part of this happy crowd? Doesn't the Bible speak of us being "encompassed about with so great a cloud of witnesses?"

She imagined Marie, thousands of miles away. Was she happy? Did she think of them, her family, as Rikka so often thought of her?

She straightened up and gave her head a little shake. Ruth's daughter Margaret ran to them and tugged at her mother's skirts. "Mama, Mama, come quick!" Rikka smiled and shooed them away.

She looked around at all these people, old and young and everything in between, each of them part of her, all in some way her family. Odin dozed in his chair. A group of youngsters played Prisoner's Base. Ole lit up another cigar. Hjordis and Gudrun sat deep in conversation. Her gaze turned to her boys, Torolf and Thorstein and Kris, laughing with Otto, as they headed to the river for a swim.

She was content.

Chapter 22

Saskatchewan, 1923

Rikka felt every one of her 62 years. She straightened her back and flexed the fingers of her left hand, wondering whether they were getting too gnarled and stiff for this delicate repetitive motion. In recent times, this had become one of her favourite chores. It would be a pity if she had to give it up. Seated at her spinning wheel on the doorstep, out of the wind and partly shaded from the sun, she felt removed from all the petty household cares that plagued her days. The pile of yarn in the basket at her side grew higher.

She looked over the fenced pasture by the barn where the flock grazed, their colours ranging from white through gray to nearly black. She felt proud that Torolf had succeeded in finding a few sheep like the ones she remembered from Norway. *Spaelsau. That's what they are called, spaelsau. The sheep we had at Karstenoya when I was a girl. The old people of the*

Their wool she prepared herself, combing out the long outer strands. Now she was spinning it into yarn. She planned to knit a weather-proof sweater to send to Kris. He wrote that although the winters in Chicago were not nearly as cold as in Saskatchewan, he found the wind and rain just as unpleasant. Spaelsau wool had kept Norwegian fishermen dry at sea for generations. It pleased Rikka to think that her son would be kept warm the same way.

Tasks like this were one of her few remaining sources of contentment.

Kris had been in Chicago for two years now, and Thorstein for almost six. None of their postwar plans had gone quite as they thought they would. There had been unexpected delays in purchasing land and livestock. Thorstein's application for entrance to a Chicago architectural college was accepted early in 1919, bringing much rejoicing but additional expenses. Rikka felt intensely grateful that Torolf and Kris had encouraged him to go.

"You are the youngest, and the only one with enough schooling to go on," Kris had said stoutly. "Marianne promises you a place to live and we will pay your tuition. I will stay and help Torolf get established here. Who knows but I might decide to become a farmer, too?"

The two young men each chose their area of management. Kris acquired land he seeded to cash crops and found plenty of off-farm employment building houses. Torolf focused his attention on livestock. Rikka no longer decided what crops to plant or how the cattle should be managed; indeed, she was seldom consulted. The homestead was hers in name only. She bowed her head and accepted this as a preordained pattern, one perhaps instituted by God Himself, or at least by His church.

Her music, however, was her own. It wounded her deeply when the all-male church council suggested she might retire as organist. Although Torolf played well, and made a fine organist, she knew his musical ability could not match her own. But how could she object that her son would succeed her? When she herself was his teacher? It was one more pain to be quietly and patiently borne, at least outwardly. Like a sliver, the slight worked its way inward.

When Torolf announced he and Ella were engaged, Kris quietly made his plans to finally move to Chicago. In the summer of 1923, Rikka's household re-created itself. Although she tried to make it plain that she was still in charge of the house, there was no denying that everyone else regarded it as primarily the home of young Torolf and his bride Ella. Rikka, mother and mother-in-law, was relegated to a status that she sometimes felt was little higher than old Inga who once had sat in her mother's chimney corner.

Ella called to her from the open window. "Shall I bring your coffee out there, Mother?"

Rikka thought, *we should take our coffee at the kaffe stua.* But she replied, "No, I will come inside." *Enough spinning for today.* She could easily finish this basket of wool tomorrow morning, the September weather promised to hold summerlike for a few more days.

It seemed that Ella had been busy in the little kitchen, enjoying a few hours of unsupervised baking while her mother-in-law worked outdoors. Rikka peered at the krumkake piled on her best platter, noting that some were too light and others a shade too dark. They should all be the same golden brown. *But she is getting better,* Rikka reminded herself. *It's never easy for two women to share a kitchen.*

She accepted a cup of coffee from Ella's hand and helped herself to a lacy brown krumkake, feeling a virtuous satisfaction that she refrained from comment. *The krumkake was certainly over-done.*

"Are you feeling better this afternoon, Ella?"

Tears filled the girl's eyes. Rikka was reminded that Ella came from a family not too shy about showing emotion. *It is a good thing that I have been acquainted all my life with her grandparents and uncles. I could not be so gentle and understanding if I did not know that Andreas and Anna will laugh aloud at lambs playing or weep over an injured sparrow. Even Marius get teary-eyed as he plays his violin.*

"Thank you for asking, Mother. I have been feeling very unwell. And sad. I had hoped that we would have a little one by this time next year. But yesterday the bleeding started. I have lost my baby."

Rikka stared at her. Never in her family were such early miscarriages spoken of. Not until at least three of a woman's monthly cycles were missed was the possibility of a child mentioned. Only after that was a miscarriage recognized, and then only because it might require medical attention.

Rikka took a long sip of her coffee and said briskly, "Well, you and Torolf are both young and healthy. Maybe you were just late, weren't really expecting a baby at all. No doubt there will be many more pregnancies. This was God's will. What was meant to be will be."

She rinsed her cup in the sink, pretending not to see the tears spilling down Ella's pale face, and hurried outside.

After covering her spinning wheel and putting the finished yarn in her basket, she walked to the hills overlooking the river. She needed the peace of the smoothly flowing river, the silence of the hills, the distant call of birds flocking for their yearly migration south. She was reluctant to return to the house. *I will give the girl time to calm herself.*

A niggling thought was rising in her mind. Maybe she was not as kind as she could be to her daughter-in-law. *But if I sympathize, that will only encourage her to feel sorry for herself,* she protested. *She must learn to be strong and stand on her own two feet. Torolf will expect her to be the capable helpmate he needs. He is clever. He has plans.*

She recalled telling herself once that marriage would be good for Torolf, make him less opinionated, maybe a little kinder. Now she had doubts.

Ella's life might well have gone in other directions. She had grown up hundreds of miles away in another province, and, following the trend of modern young women of the 1920s, had left her parents' farm to find work "in the city". She studied at a business college, was employed as a comptometer operator in a big office building and wore bloomers to play riotous games of basketball with other young ladies of Edmonton. Rikka had listened in stunned silence when Ella boasted of that.

"Our team was so good we hardly ever lost a game!"

On a holiday to visit her grandparents Anna and Andreas in Saskatchewan, she happened to accompany her uncle Marius and aunt Signe to Rikka's house for their customary Sunday afternoon music. Marius brought his violin, Rikka and Torolf alternated on piano, Kris on cornet, a half dozen others came with their instruments and their fine singing voices. Rikka noticed that Ella did not offer to play. Although she sang along softly, it seemed she was only mouthing the words.

Torolf noticed only her blue eyes smiling up at him from under brows like angel wings.

Rikka wondered whether the magic of those gentle eyes could survive his irritation at kohlrabi mistaken for cabbage, for krumkake cooked a shade too brown, for weeping in the kitchen.

He expects her to be like me. As soon as the thought came to her, she realized the truth of it. With no example of a kindly father to guide his childhood and adolescence, he had not learned gentleness or sympathy for the women in his life. He, like Kris, had been critical and unforgiving of any weakness displayed by his sisters. He took with only perfunctory thanks what his mother gave him, from his favourite dessert to her only farm.

He has a quick mind and a stubborn determination, like his father. And he feels as uncomfortable as I do when confronted by displays of emotion. She saw, as though in a picture, the life Ella would lead with Torolf.

He will forever be proving himself. She must either make his dreams and projects her own or she will be shut out.

"Would we all have been different, if you had lived, Mentz?" She cried the words aloud, then looked around, fearful someone might have heard her anguish.

Of course, no one will hear, there is no one but me. Me and God, alone on the hill. Alone. As always.

She walked slowly across the dry grass and stopped at the paddock to pump water for the sheep.

Mentz would have taught by example, demonstrating kindness. It was up to her now. She made a promise, to herself or to God or to Mentz, she was not sure which. She vowed to do whatever she could to make life more pleasant for Ella.

She promised to do what she could.

In the end, that seemed to amount to very little. Torolf continued to pursue his varied interests with single-minded determination. He might be gone for a week at a time, visiting an experimental farm or attending an agricultural conference. Rikka and Ella accepted without comment the barnyard chores that were left in their hands. Torolf was, after all, a very busy man. In addition to serving as the church organist he was a fixture in every choir or quartet in their community. Most Sunday afternoons, the group of amateur musicians continued to meet at the homestead in the valley. The impromptu little orchestra was often called upon to play during silent motion pictures in Elbow's Wynn Theatre. Rikka was pleased with the cultured atmosphere they created. Ella was pleased they played loudly enough to mask the annoying racket of projector gears.

Rikka tried her best to become more a mother and less a mother-in-law to Ella. That did not often yield the desired results. Despite constant and, in Rikka's opinion, extremely patient instruction, Ella did not become a skilful knitter nor an indefatigable gardener. Ella remained Ella. Her piecrust was tough, but her angel cake topnotch. While Torolf read veterinary manuals and horticulture books, Ella read novels and women's magazines. Rikka discovered to her consternation that she even wrote a little poetry. She did not play the piano. Although she enjoyed the choir, no one suggested she sing a solo for "special music" at church. Rikka gave up and decided to love the girl as she was.

After that life in the little house in the valley was happier.

Chapter 23

Saskatchewan, 1925-28

Rikka straightened her aching back and found her daughter-in-law doing likewise. Rikka called across the garden, "Just another half hour and then we'll be finished."

The potatoes had to be hilled, aching back or not. The hot July sun would turn the tubers green and unusable. That was waste they could not afford.

They finally finished and were trudging back to the house when Torolf drove into the yard. He hopped down from the wagon and called, "Put the coffee on while I stable the horses. I have some big news to tell you."

It was news that Rikka had been expecting for the past year. Although none of them spoke of it, she suspected Ella, at least, felt as she did. The little farmhouse was inadequate for them. It must have become equally obvious to Torolf that the 160 acres of her original homestead could never support the family he hoped to have.

As they gathered around the kitchen table, coffee cups in hand, Torolf pealed a paper out of his pocketbook and smoothed it on the wooden table so that both women could see the name of a land company. Rikka recognised the letterhead from ads in the local paper.

"I have bought myself a farm," he announced. "It has a house ready-built, almost brand new. Not more than a dozen miles from here. You will recognise the place, Mama, you can see it from Fagerheim."

"Where ..." asked Ella, but Torolf interrupted her. "You know, Ella, I pointed it out to you once, Fagerheim is the farm where Uncle Odin lived. Our new farm is just south of that. And it is only a few miles down the road from Ruth and Walter's place, too."

As though to prevent more questions, he hurried on.

"We will keep this place of course. It's good summer pasture for the cattle. But I want to concentrate on building up a herd of Aberdeen Angus. The black ones."

"When ...?" Ella began but was again cut off.

"We can move right away. I'd like to get settled in our new place before harvest. Breaking needs to be done before winter, too."

He continued in a reassuring tone. "Mama, you can keep on living here as long as you like. You can have your chickens and your garden and your flowers and so on."

He stopped suddenly. "Oh, I almost forgot. The station agent caught me just as I was leaving town, said there was a telegram for you, Ella. I guess I left it in the wagon."

Ella followed him out of the house. Rikka stood in the doorway watching as Torolf rummaged in the storage box they kept under the wagon seat and finally produced a square envelope. Ella tore it open and burst into tears.

Torolf took it from her, scanned it quickly and turned to Rikka. "It's from her father. Her mother died yesterday."

As Rikka hurried to embrace Ella - *Is this really the first time I have hugged her? -* she heard Torolf say, in a curiously detached tone, "And he wants her to bring her little sister Edith to live with us."

In the weeks that followed, Rikka felt as though she were revisiting all the emotions of her years in Teulon. Ella was devastated by the death of her mother who, at 48, had seemed in the prime of her life. Ella's uncle Adolph and grandmother Anna travelled with Ella by train to Alberta for the funeral. Adolph and Anna would come back the next week but Ella, would stay a little longer with her bereaved father and grieving siblings. In her absence, Torolf was pulled in every direction by the demands of this busiest time in a farm season. It was left to Rikka to pack his and Ella's belongings and orchestrate the move. During the hottest days of summer, she drove her buggy from the valley homestead to the new farm two or three times a week, setting up Torolf and Ella's home while emptying her own. Ruth often came to help, along with her children, 12-year-old Margaret and 3-year-old Noble.

"It will be so nice to have Ella and Torolf living just a hop and a skip away from us." Ruth paused in her scrubbing of mouse dirt from the kitchen cupboards. She stepped out the door and carefully emptied the pail of dirty water around the hollyhocks Rikka had transplanted from her garden, then refilled the pail from the pump in the mudroom. "When our menfolk are away, she and I can run back and forth whenever we want a visit. Ella's little sister will be at school with Margaret. They won't be lonely."

Ruth has always had a kind heart, thought Rikka. Aloud she said, "Torolf will be glad that you keep an eye on them."

"Oh, we'll be good company for each other! And you know, my Walter needs help with harvest so I wrote to Ella that she should bring her brother to work for us. He is only 17 but a good worker. I know he will be missing his Mama. It would be nice for him to be close to his sisters. A change of scene will help, too."

When Ella stepped off the train, a small blond girl clung to her hand and a tall shy teenage boy came behind carrying their bags. Ella's brother Oscar had decided at the last minute to accept Ruth and Walter's offer. Torolf and Ella and young Edith were settled in their new home before summer waned. The few dusty miles that separated their farm from Ruth and Walter's was nothing to people comfortable with riding or walking miles every day. After evening chores were done, Oscar often appeared at Ella's door – "I can smell that you have the coffee on!" Ruth and Margaret never missed a Sunday afternoon visit with Ella and Edith. Ella's life had become full as Rikka's emptied.

For the first time in her life Rikka was alone.

She discovered an unexpected pleasure in planning her day as she pleased. She fed her ducks and geese, dug the potatoes, piling the biggest and best in the wagon to fill Torolf's new root cellar. She took her coffee outside to the kaffe stua and watched the sunrise. She laughed aloud at a family of prairie chickens enjoying a dust bath. She stood still for long minutes, scanning the sky and listening to migrating flocks passing far overhead. At dusk, she paused in her doorway to hear the coyotes' serenade before calling her old dog inside for the night. She went to church and attended village socials and welcomed Sunday afternoon visitors coming to make music at her house. The seasons slipped by, even more quickly than in past years.

* * *

She was not lonely.

But when she saw Ruth's horse and buggy coming up the trail, she smiled. *It will be nice to have coffee together, just the two of us.* She finished gathering the eggs and carried the basket to the house. Ruth hopped down from the buggy and hugged her.

"Mama, I've come to take you on a picnic!"

After confirming that Ruth had indeed brought coffee, in a quart sealer, the jar wrapped well in tea towels to keep it hot, and after fetching her own warm jacket in case the day turned chilly, and after grumbling, for the sake of propriety, "Whoever heard of a picnic in October! And without the children!" Rikka climbed into the buggy beside her daughter. "Well now, you had better tell me where we are going. And why!"

Ruth slapped the reins on the horse's rump and grinned, her mischievous expression erasing the years, making her look to Rikka like the child she had so often scolded. "I am taking you to a place you have never been before. I want to introduce you to an old friend of mine."

"Ruth, I am not fit for company! You must take me home so I can change."

"No, no Mama, it's alright, my friend is very old and very wise and will not even notice what you are wearing."

There was a seriousness behind Ruth's bantering tone that puzzled Rikka. She felt even more puzzled when, after following a trail for a few miles down the valley, Ruth turned the buggy onto a track that seemed to lead into a large pasture.

"Here we are, Mama. Come and meet my friend." Ruth scrambled to the ground with the picnic basket and reached up to give her mother a hand down. "It's just a short walk across level prairie from here."

Rikka looked around, trying to guess their destination. No house in sight, not even a tree close by, just short prairie grass and what looked at first glance like a haystack. As they strolled towards it, Rikka realized the haystack was in fact a large rock, a boulder, set like a solitary sentinel on the open plain, incongruously alone. *Like me*, thought Rikka. *It has settled here but does not quite belong.*

"I know," she exclaimed. "It is the buffalo rock Margaret and Noble chattered on about."

"You guessed right! Walter took me here for the first time when we were courting. In fact, it was here I told him he must marry me! We like to come back when we have time. The children think it is a magical place. Margaret wondered how it happened you didn't know about it."

Ruth spread a blanket on the sunny side of the big rock, and they sat down. "I told her that you always had so many of your own people to look after, you had not had time to meet your other neighbours."

Ruth sat up straight, and, taking her mother's hand, she pressed it against the sun-warmed rock. "Buffalo Rock, Guardian of your valley, meet my mother, Rikka of the kaffe stua tree, also in your valley."

Rikka's first impulse was to protest at this foolishness and pull away; but the rock's surface was warm and comforting and so was Ruth's voice. Without thinking, she nodded graciously to the rock, as though she had indeed been presented to an old and venerable member of the community.

Then she laughed self-consciously, wondering how Ruth was able by her matter-of-factness to make even talking to a rock seem normal. "Why do you call it the guardian of the valley?"

"Just a name I gave it. I think it must have been important to other people who lived here in times past. If you come here when the grass has been grazed short, you can see circles of rocks all around it outlining where people set their tipis, and rows of rock marking pathways. It is sad we don't know its history. I am sure people came here to pray – can't you feel the spirits all around us?"

I should have stopped Ruth from thinking like that when she was a little girl, Rikka scolded herself. Aloud she said, "People will think you are hardly Christian, with your talk of spirits!"

Ruth laughed. "But you are not 'people', Mama, you are my own dear mother, and you know I cannot help how I am. I can feel the presence of spirits. And I want you to meet this dear friend. While we still have time."

Rikka relaxed against the stone, feeling the warmth seep into her spine, and smiled. "Well, as for having time, I seem to have lots of it these days. And your friend the Buffalo Rock is not going anywhere."

"No." said Ruth, "but I am."

Rikka sat bolt upright. "Why? What happened?"

"You know Walter has been restless. He has always hated the winters, wanted to move somewhere he never has to fight snow. Well, now I have agreed that we should leave. Not because I want to but because I think it will be better for us and for my family."

Rikka's voice sounded fearful, even to her. "Does it have to do with Adolph's fire?"

The fire. Rikka had been shocked to learn at church that Marius' brother Adolph had suffered a devastating loss on his farm. A talented machinist, he had invested all his savings to build a modern machine shop where he was rumoured to be building his own gas-powered tractor. Ten days ago, everything - tractor, tools, machine shop - had been destroyed in a blaze. Rikka had driven out to his farm as soon as she heard about it to offer sympathy. After all, she had known him since he was a boy in Vikna, his brother was married to her niece, and he was her daughter-in-law Ella's uncle. In their complex tangle of relationships, he was family. But he had refused to come to the door, had not answered her repeated knock, although she felt sure he was home.

Ruth nodded, her eyes filling with tears. "It was awful. Walter came home so upset, hands burned and clothes smelling of smoke. I thought, at first, he had been helping fight the fire and of course, he had been. But it was worse. Earlier that evening he had stopped to see the man Adolph hired to help around the farm, and they got to drinking. Pretty soon the bottle was empty, so the fellow says, come on, we'll take Adolph's car into town and go to the pub, he won't mind. The car was out of gas, so they took a lantern into the machine shop to fill a can with gas …"

"And the fools set fire to the place." Rikka's face was grim.

Ruth nodded. "Adolph won't come out of his house or talk to anyone. His hired man hightailed it out of the country. Walter is so ashamed, he cannot face Ella or any of the family. He wants to tell Adolph how sorry he is but Adolph won't talk to him. There is no way he can make it right. He thinks it would be better for Adolph if we just left the country. It's what he has always wanted to do anyway, move to Arizona."

"Yes, I see. Thank you, Ruth, for telling me. It could not have been easy."

"I could not go without explaining it all to you, Mama. And I really did want to introduce you to my old friend here, the buffalo rock. Don't you feel the power, the peace? I know people have been bringing their prayers here for hundreds of years. Margaret and Noble poked sticks into the cracks in the rock and pulled out bits of cloth and carved bone and coloured glass beads put there who knows how long ago. I always made them put them back. Prayers should be respected."

She pulled a beaded bracelet from her pocket and tucked it into a crack in the buffalo rock. "I made this bracelet to leave as an offering and a prayer. May the guardian of this valley always look after my mother."

Rikka hugged her tight. "And may the good Lord protect you and your family, wherever you go."

Within a month, Ruth and her family had left the farm they were renting to seek a new life in a new country.

* * *

In the following years, Rikka drove into town every week to pick up the mail, hoping for a letter from one of her daughters living in the United States. She was seldom disappointed. It gave her pleasure to write to Ruth that Adolph had made a miraculous recovery from his depression. Some weeks before the fire, an agent of a farm equipment company had visited Adolph's farm, seen the prototype of Adolph's machine, and brought back a description to his boss in the states. When the letter arrived offering Adolph work designing equipment in their factory, he smiled again. He sold his farm and moved south of the border.

It seems my whole life has been filled with family and old friends escaping to another land, Rikka mused. The thought did not make her sad. All life was change. Although she herself wanted no more

301

disruptions, she accepted them as inevitable. Babies would be born, children would grow up, friends would fall out or grow fonder, marriages would thrive or fail. She tried to place herself to help wherever she could. She felt content with the few friends who still came to visit, and the growing number of grandchildren who made her house glad at Christmas and Easter. She was largely removed from the petty aggravations of her family's daily lives and took at face value their assurances all was well. That was enough.

They refrained from burdening her with details of financial or marital hardship; she never mentioned her shortness of breath or the recurring stitch in her side.

It was late summer, 1928. She had spent the previous week at Torolf and Ella's home, canning garden vegetables and putting up preserves in preparation for harvest. With a year-old toddler and newborn baby, Ella's hands were full. *It's a lucky thing that they brought Edith to live with them,* thought Rikka. In the five years she had been with them, Ella's little sister had matured from a needy child to a valuable helper. Ella's kitchen was far too small for all the cooking, preserving, and meat-cutting done there; but long practise enabled the women to work together in the cramped space. As Rikka turned from the stove, she saw that Edith had started moving the cooling quart sealers from the kitchen table to the shelf in the mudroom. *Good! Now I will just empty this canner of hot water out the door, and we can start supper.* Using towels to protect her hands, she gripped the hot canner firmly by its side-handles, turned and took a step towards the door.

She was never sure afterwards whether it was Edith's cry of alarm or some sixth sense that made her pause, foot in air. The sudden realization that she had almost tripped over her small grandson turned her bones to milk. Trembling, she barely was able to stay on her feet long enough for Edith to take the canner of boiling water from her.

She sank into a chair, unable to utter a sound. *Pull yourself together, woman! The child is not hurt. Stop imagining what might have happened if ...* Her breath came in gasps and the pressure rising in her chest was unbearable. Edith had scooped up little Len and put him in his highchair at the table out of harms way. Ella, who had been nursing the baby in the next room, appeared in the doorway, alarm written on her face. Rikka forced what she hoped was a brisk tone and said, "No harm done, thank heaven!"

But the harm had been done. She was still pale and breathless when the men came in for supper. Torolf insisted on taking her the next day to see the doctor. He had a long discussion with the doctor after Rikka left the consulting room, and emerged looking severe, his typical expression when worried. Rikka decided this was altogether too much fuss for something that could be chalked up to old age.

"I have your preserves and baking ready for the threshing crew when they come," she said. "My own garden needs attention. It is high time I go back to my own place now and get it ready for another winter."

That simply would not do, her children decided in a flurry of letters to and from Arizona and Chicago and Saskatchewan. It seemed that for the first time they saw her slower gait, her bent shoulders, her advanced years. Instead of the mother who had been their bulwark and strength she had become their problem. What to do with Mama? Rikka made it plain that she had no intention of moving into either Hjordis' or Torolf's cramped and crowded households. As for her daughters who had moved to the States, well, Marie and Ruth were no more eager for their mother to come to live with them than Rikka was to go. That left Kris and Thorstein, both settled and thriving in Chicago. Thorstein had married and had a young son. Only Kris was, as yet, unattached.

Kris wrote to her. "At least come for a visit, Mama. You have not met Thorstein's wife, whom you will be sure to like. Marie and Ruth could easily make the trip to Chicago to visit you, and you know Marianne would welcome you with open arms. You may find this feels more like home than you expect."

Rikka almost laughed. Had not wherever she went become somehow her home? She had poured out her youth and passion at Vikna, her agony and grief into the swampy fields of Teulon, her determination and hope into this prairie farm. She had left a piece of herself behind every time she moved. Why should not Chicago become home, too, when the biggest and best part of her lay moldering in a cemetery there these past twenty years?

Chapter 24

Chicago – 1928

"But tell me, how are you, Aunt Rikka?"

"Oh, Fine, I am fine. Nothing to complain of."

"You never were one for complaining, were you."

Rikka looked up into a gaze as uncompromising as her own. "No, why should one complain? The good Lord knows what we can take and never gives us more than we can bear ..."

"Hogwash! Haven't you ever wanted to scream, 'Stop, I can't take any more?' I know I have!"

They had been speaking only English until this point, but Marianne's outburst was in old country Norwegian.

The pain in Rikka's throat returned, making it impossible to reply. She shook her head.

"But you know what I have learned, Aunt Rikka? It is not really the terrible things that happen to us that are unbearable. It is all the awfulness that we deny, the pain we don't acknowledge. That is what can poison our lives."

"Yes, yes, you are right. No doubt our own actions cause most of our pain. Sin brings consequences." Rikka had found her voice again, insisting by her return to English that old times were to be spoken of only in generalities. She resumed the formal distant tone she had used when Marianne first entered the apartment.

Marianne smiled a smile as insincere as Rikka's tone and shrugged. The conversation turned to news about mutual acquaintances and friends of the family. Marianne asked after her cousins and half brothers and sisters in Canada, and Rikka gave details of births, deaths, and marriages. Eventually every relationship had been covered. It seemed there was nothing more to say.

Marianne glanced at her watch, exclaimed at the lateness of the afternoon, gathered her handbag and coat and adjusted her jaunty little hat.

As she went through the doorway, she turned and grasped Rikka's hand.

"It's alright, Aunt Rikka, to be sad. But don't blame yourself. Or me. We all did the best we could at the time."

Shaken, Rikka closed the door behind her sister's daughter. Suddenly the little apartment with its dingy linoleum floor and harsh electric lighting and pervasive odour of gas felt unbearable. With trembling hands, she took her long black coat off the hook by the door and let herself out, remembering just in time to pocket the key before the door locked behind her. She hurried down the stairs and out into dull autumn sunshine. There was a park just a few blocks away, where children played on swings and old men sat on park benches. She could walk those gravel paths as invisible as a ghost. No one there would know her. She could let herself remember.

Remember all the things she could not forget.

* * *

Rikka walked slowly. The park was only a short distance away, but her legs felt heavy and weary as though she had been walking uphill for a very long time. The rain clouds that threatened earlier now scudded across the sky away from the lake. She was reminded of Kris's admonition – "You should always carry an umbrella. It might rain at anytime in Chicago, Mama," – and smiled to herself. When had she ever been afraid of getting wet? And if it really was a storm to be feared, what good was a flimsy umbrella?

A little rain never hurt anyone. And there is no protection against real storms.

She at last reached the park's sedate wrought iron gate. A child was chasing his hoop down the gravelled path towards her, and she stepped aside. He bounded past her, followed by a young woman who smiled and said something vaguely apologetic. Rikka nodded her head curtly, thinking nurse? Governess? His mother? She felt ill at ease in this place, not knowing by name any of the people she met or where they fit into the ramshackle social structure that made up this urban community.

She thought about the community of her childhood, where everyone knew everyone else, each had a predetermined place, accepted by all. *They knew me and I knew them and their families. For generations back, our families were known to each other. Mentz came into that place and made it his own, through his honesty and hard work. He earned it. My family was already known, we were born to the place, our position was secure.*

Strange how I never understood that until I became a stranger in another land and had nothing. No resources beyond my own strength, no position in the community, no respect owed to me or mine.

She felt again the panicked aloneness she had experienced on the homestead in Teulon.

Rikka forced herself to remember the days and months and years when she could expect no help, no sympathy, no support beyond the courtesy of her neighbours. Courtesy, or charity. Charity. She cringed at the word.

My children died and I could not even pay for markers on their graves.

She choked back the sob that rose from deep inside and forced herself to walk, erect and deliberate, towards a vacant bench. Here a line of spruce trees blocked the chill wind and hid her from view. She sat with her coat pulled tight over her knees. Marianne's parting words came back to her.

"It's alright, Aunt Rikka, to be sad. But don't blame yourself. Or me. We all did the best we could at the time."

But that's just the problem, you see. You can never know if you did your best. I might have worked harder, prayed better, loved more. Everything might have been different. I might never have had to bear this terrible self-doubt, this pain that I carry with me wherever I go.

What else had Marianne said? Something about pain working inward. Ah yes now she remembered. She could almost see Marianne standing before her, no pity but immense understanding shining from her eyes.

"But you know what I have learned, Aunt Rikka? It is not really the terrible things that happen to us that are unbearable. It is all the awfulness that we deny, the pain we don't acknowledge. That is what can poison our lives."

Has the pain I carry hidden in me poisoned my life? Did self-blame work its way into my soul like a piece of glass? Wounding and blinding me?

She had to admit that it was so. The nagging thought she might have prevented her brother's death if she had confronted him, when she heard the clank of bottles that he carried aboard that ill-fated voyage; her resentment of Marianne; the self-blame that followed the death of Marianne's child – she had kept it all hidden, ashamed to show her weakness. *If I had brought it out into the light of day, it might be that Mother and Kristine and Mentz would have shown me it was nonsense. Even our old Pastor might have advised me to confess it to God and be done with it.*

Hidden deep within, it had poisoned her life, robbed her of joy. It had poisoned her love for Mentz, turning her love into jealousy. She saw it all as from a great distance, removed, detached from her old self. She saw herself becoming bent and twisted under the burden. And she felt only wonder and pity for the foolish woman she was, hanging onto her useless pain despite the compassionate wounded hand extended to take it from her.

Why did I inflict it on myself? I sat like Job in the ashes of my grief, scraping at my sores.

The terrible things that happened - and they were terrible! How awful the death of one child! And another and another and another - so terrible, so unendurable, and yet that grief and loss and sorrow was like a clean surgical wound when compared to that old festering sore of self blame. I piled the deaths of my children onto the load of guilt I already carried.

And yet. Even in those darkest times, we had each other. Mentz knew he could count on me, even at my worst, to do my best. And even when I did not agree with him, when he seemed to put everything else before me, I knew he would do almost anything for me and our children. He would lay down his life for us, but not his integrity.

The words came into her mind as though she were not reading them in his last letter but hearing him speak those words to her for the first time.

"Without which I cannot live."

And she realized that Mentz's words meant something more than she had understood. Their love, at once so imperfect and so pure, was part of the Big Love, the eternal sacred flame that brought the world into being and sustained everything worth having. Mentz's stubborn forgiving devotion to her was part and parcel of who he was. It was bound up with his tenderness for his children, his compassion for others, for the world itself. It could not be changed or taken away, even by death. She loved him as she always would love him, so long as she had breath, and afterwards too, because they were both part of that one immense love that filled the universe and created life and sustained hope and would never end. She felt breathless yet exhilarated, as though she had been running for a very long time and was at last reaching home.

"Without which I cannot live."

She saw it all now, saw it clearly. *"Without which I cannot live."* She stood up and hurried along the path, wanting to laugh and cry and say to Mentz, "Yes, I see! I see! I am the same, I too cannot live without it. I give you my love, and you give it to me. No, that's not quite right – it is more like when we picked berries together, when we were young and new to life. We plucked the ripest juiciest berries, all given to us freely by sunshine and rain, as though from the Lord's own hand, and saved the best for each other. Our love was like that. We took from all the love that surrounded us - from your parents, my mother, from our families and our church, our community and neighbours and friends, the wild sea and clean air, the strong mountains and green trees - all gifts from God - and shared it with each other. As our spirits grew strong, we gave back through our work and our family and our music. Our love."

Her pace slowed again as she searched her memory for all who had been a part of her life. Faces flashed through her mind, an immense cloud of witnesses. Her mother, Kristine and Kris. Pastor Olson, her music teachers, all their household and friends and neighbours at Vikna. The Baptist community at Teulon. Strangers, people she never knew, who helped Mentz in Chicago. The little Norwegian congregation who had protected her dignity and renewed her spirit with music. Her children. All so flawed, all so precious.

And Marianne, who cared for Marie and Ruth, Thorstein and Kris, as though they were her own.

But it all began long before that, maybe at the very beginning of the world. God wove love into the fabric of the universe. We exist in an ocean of love. The spirit grows strong by feeding on love freely given and then out of sheer joy giving it back. Giving without ever knowing how it will end. That is the root and the heart of it all ...

A golden ray of autumn sun broke through the clouds low in the western sky and dappled the path before her with the shadows of naked trees. Among all the bare branches, a lone ash tree blazed in the light, still clothed in late autumn hues of purple and red. Rikka stopped before it and clasped her hands, suddenly overwhelmed with grief and joy at its beauty. *Yes, that is the root and the heart of it all. Like this old tree, blazing with colour before sleeping for a time, maybe returning to life in the spring, maybe not, but for now giving its all. As Mentz gave his all. For me. For his children. How did I fail to see that? He loved me. As I loved him.*

And as Marianne loved him.

She hurried along the path, tottering in her haste, oblivious of the wind whipping her hair loose from its coiled braid.

She desperately longed to hold on to that vision. She felt terribly afraid that it would fade before she dared act on it.

First of all, she and Marianne must talk.

The End

Joan Soggie's lifelong curiosity about her homeland has led her to explore the native prairie, the centuries-long relationship between the land and First Nations, and her own family's settler history. Her earlier writings include regional histories *Mistaseni: A Story of the Buffalo Rock of Elbow* and *Looking for Aiktow: Stories Behind the History of the Elbow of the South Saskatchewan River,* and historical fiction, *Prairie Grass*, published by BWL Publishing Inc., 2020

The prairie and all its creatures are her inspiration. Her family is her joy. She and her husband, Dennis, treasure days with their children, grandchildren, and great-grandchildren. Joan Soggie lives and writes in rural Saskatchewan

Made in the USA
Monee, IL
17 December 2024

74121719R00185